COMANCHE MOON

Banner had to confront the fear that had haunted him for five long years, but only a fool would dare to venture back to the Lost River stronghold and challenge the might of Ghost Warrior's Comanche horde again. Every Comanche eye would be looking for him and every Comanche arrow had his name on it. Did Banner have the courage to face up to the tremendous odds stacked against him or had he left his nerve back there. Only Banner could decide, but a young girl's life and future depended on his decision.

COMANCHE MOON

For Zara,
And all the joy you gave

COMANCHE MOON

by
John Brand

Dales Large Print Books
Long Preston, North Yorkshire,
England.

British Library Cataloguing in Publication Data.

Brand, John
    Comanche moon.

    A catalogue record for this book is
    available from the British Library

    ISBN 1-85389-898-8 pbk

First published in Great Britain by Robert Hale Ltd., 1997

Cover illustration © Lopez by arrangement with Norma
Editorial S.A.

Published in Large Print 1999 by arrangement with Robert
Hale Ltd.

Dales Large Print is an imprint of
Library Magna Books Ltd.
Printed and bound in Great Britain by
T.J. International Ltd., Cornwall, PL28 8RW.

1

Silence descended abruptly on the dimly lit cantina as the three strangers entered; only the echoes of a Mexican love song remained as the player put aside his guitar. Once more the deathly moaning of the wind could be heard in the deserted street. Somewhere in that dark night a dog whined in terror at the growling thunder.

Fear had become a tangible thing in the cantina also as the half-dozen customers moved swiftly aside to make room for the newcomers, each of those customers wishing he were out in that dark lonely street heading for the safety of his home.

Paco, the bartender, shrugged mentally. He was accustomed to such things, but always with the taste of fear in his mouth. He did not like that taste. Who could tell what men such as these would do?

Many such men crossed the Rio Bravo and found themselves in the village with no name. It was the price one had to pay for living so close to the border. Sometimes the cowboys came to spend their hard-earned money on the ever-willing *señoritas*, but usually it was the *pistoleros* and *banditos* who came to hide from the gringo law across the Rio Grande. Sometimes they came to rob and kill with little fear for the outcome of their actions. The *federales* cared nothing for the safety of those who could not afford the price of protection.

Already the eldest of the three men had shown his contempt for the others by removing his slicker and moving to the far end of the bar with the Mexicans. Steam rose from his rain-soaked pants as he neared the stone fireplace. The healthy glow of the fire brought a smile to his face.

'Only one thing better than a hot fire on a cold night, and that's a warm woman,' he said to no one in particular, but winking at Paco. 'A bottle of your best and a glass, amigo.'

Paco obliged quickly. This man he liked. He had an open, friendly face that told Paco he had nothing to fear from him. Taking the bottle and glass, the elderly man seated himself in the over-stuffed armchair near the fire, the chair favoured by so many of Paco's customers.

Paco edged closer to the other men, not liking what he saw. He had seen their type before. Hired guns! The young man with the red hair was very dangerous. Unless Paco missed his guess, this youth needed no reason to kill.

Forcing a smile on to his unwilling face, Paco sidled up to the two men. 'Good evening, señors. Welcome to Paco's Cantina. How may I serve you?'

'First, a couple of whiskies,' the taller of the two men said. 'Second, we need a little information. We're looking for a man calling himself Banner. We were told you might know where we can find him.'

Somehow Paco managed to avoid glancing towards the darkened end of the long room. As dangerous as these two men were, the man called Banner was much more dangerous, although Paco knew he had nothing to fear from him. This the whole village knew.

The man at the fire shaved Bull Durham into his old pipe and grinned.

'You real sure you want to find him, Kirby? It could be a mistake. Probably your last.'

Kirby removed his wet slicker, placing it alongside Red's on the highly polished bar. Paco winced. That bar was his pride and joy. Every spare moment was spent polishing that rich wood.

'You talk too much, Cody,' Kirby snapped. 'Makes me wonder how you got to be so old. Don't know why the major ordered you to come with us, but nothing was said about bringing you back. As far as I'm concerned once we find Banner your job is finished. Understand, Cody?'

Despite the threat, Cody remained relaxed as he puffed on his old pipe. 'Nobody ordered me to come along, Kirby. I don't work for Buckman, remember? I tagged along because I wanted to see what happened when you come up against Banner. He doesn't take orders from anyone, and that includes the major.' He grinned suddenly. 'Tell you something else, Kirby ... right now, I got more chance of recrossing the Rio than you have.'

'He'll come with us, Cody. We have our own methods of persuasion. He'll be glad to come with us. You are going to find out that Banner isn't as tough as you think he is.'

He turned his attention back to little Paco, the anger burning in his eyes. 'You haven't answered my question yet, amigo.'

'Señor Banner lives high in the mountains, *señor*,' Paco answered softly. 'He does not come to the village very often. It is said that he does not like company.'

For the first time, the red-haired youth spoke, his voice bristling with the aggression of many small men. 'We don't give a damn what Banner likes. We're here to find him, and you are going to tell us just where he is. *Comprende?*'

'I regret that I must respect his wishes, *señor*. If you wish, I will send someone to meet up with him and ask if he would like to see you. I regret this is all I can do.'

Paco felt proud of himself and his newly found courage. He would be the talk of the village. No one had ever spoken thus to two gunmen and lived to tell of it.

Already his *compadres* were watching him with undisguised admiration. As soon as the gringos left they would hurry to the homes of their families and friends to tell of the bravery of little Paco. His fame would spread to the other villages and he would become a hero.

A proud smile touched the corners of his mouth. All his life he had wanted to be a hero; and now his dream had come true

... but the dream was to be short-lived.

Kirby seemed unaware of Paco's defiance as he studied the sign above the bar mirror. 'That your name on the sign, amigo?'

'*Si, señor.* I am the prop ... prop ... owner of Paco's Cantina.'

'That's one hell of a handle, amigo,' Kirby said, studying the long sign. 'Think it will all fit on a tombstone, Red?'

A wolfish grin split Red's features. He had worked with Kirby for a few years now and knew how his mind worked. 'Won't leave much room for the dates, Kirby. Best to keep it short. Paco born ... when were you born, greaser?'

Paco told him quietly, his voice barely audible.

'Paco died ... what is today's date, Kirby?'

Paco swallowed hard, trying to draw breath into his oxygen starved body. The cold cramp of fear tightened in his stomach. The village would no longer speak of Paco, the hero; instead they would speak of Paco, the fool, and lament his passing.

There was little doubt now that the men intended to kill him, even if he gave them the information they sought. His death would serve as an example to any other who might defy them. One of the other men in the cantina would provide them with the information they needed and little Paco's death would be meaningless.

A match flared suddenly in the darkened corner of the room and the gringos became aware of another presence in the room. Paco felt relief flood through him, leaving him weak. For the moment he had forgotten the big man who liked to sit alone in his dark corner, and think his own dark thoughts.

He learned to breathe again as the tall, wide shouldered man eased himself to his feet and moved towards the bar. Gratefully, Paco filled a glass with beer. The *señor* rarely drank spirits. He sighed. Thanks to the *señor* there would be no sorrow in Paco's home tonight.

Kirby relaxed. If his guess was right, this was the man they were looking for. Maybe this was going to be one of the easy jobs. At least, they had avoided a trip to the mountains. He had the feeling that Banner would have been a hard man to find up there.

'Your name Banner?' Kirby asked.

'Who's asking?' the tall man asked.

'The name's Kirby. My friend there is called Red, Cody told us you would be a hard man to find. He was wrong.'

'He wasn't wrong: I made it easy for you. I've known about you ever since you crossed the Rio. I wanted to know why a couple of two-bit gunmen were looking for me.'

Kirby held up a restraining hand as Red moved away from the bar. The kid had a hair-trigger temper, and had killed for less provocation.

'We've got a job to do first, Red. You can settle with him when it's all over.'

He turned his attention back to Banner.

'We would have found you, Banner. Maybe it would have taken a little longer, but when Major Buckman gives us a job to do we get it done. Right now, our job is to take you back to him.'

'And if I don't want to go?' Banner asked quietly.

'We've got our orders. We always follow orders.'

Banner sipped at his beer, holding the glass in his left hand as he glanced at Cody.

'What's your part in this, Cody?'

'Personal, Banner. I figured on talking to you after the funerals.'

'That big mouth of yours is going to get you killed, Cody,' Red snapped, still seething from Banner's remark about two-bit gunmen. Banner would pay for that.

'The major has a job for you, Banner. A big job by the kind of money he's offering. Ten thousand dollars. That's a lot of money. Got anything against money, Banner?'

'Depends on how a man uses it,' Banner said softly. 'Go back to your major and tell him I'm not interested.'

'The major doesn't like taking no for an answer. He might think we have failed him. He won't like that and neither do we.'

'You have,' Banner said easily.

'Money doesn't interest you, Banner? Or maybe you are just plain scared of the job the major is offering you? I can understand that. I don't know just what the job is, Banner, neither does Red. We think that Cody knows, but he isn't talking either.'

'Maybe they don't trust you,' Banner said.

'There's only one other man working for Buckman better with a gun than Red and me, but he hasn't got the brains that I've got, or the patience. Jack Stagg would have probably killed you by now. He doesn't like anyone saying no to him. Red is just itching to kill you but I can't let that happen—yet.'

He stopped talking long enough to light a cigarette. 'The job he has in mind, the one he won't talk about, he seems to think you are the only man for it. I don't know why he should think that, but I believe Cody had something to do with it. Tell me, Banner, what makes you so special?'

'Maybe the fact that I can't be bought,' Banner said easily. His response rattled Kirby. He was taking a long hard look at Banner now and not liking what he saw. There was a cool easy confidence in the man that disturbed him. Who the hell was Banner anyway? That was another secret that Cody held close to his chest. He had to be someone. Had to. Men as tough as Banner didn't suddenly appear out of nowhere. There had to be a past. Any man who could face up to two gunmen without any trace of doubt or fear had to have a reputation but, until a few days ago, he had never even heard of anyone named Banner.

There had to be another name. Some-where along the line Banner had changed his name. That was the only answer. Desperately, Kirby began searching his memory for another name to fit Banner's description. He was beginning to feel what little Paco had felt a few minutes ago and didn't like it. Sweat popped on his brow. He needed time to think. Maybe the wisest course would be for them to back off and ride away. This was beginning to smell like big trouble. That option was taken from him by Red. The boy was chomping at the bit. Banner calling him a two-bit gunslick had riled him beyond reason. Only Banner's notch on his gunbutt would satisfy him now.

'We're wasting time, Kirby. I say we take Banner back with us, no matter how. Face down across a saddle will suit me just fine. Nobody can say we failed then. My way we get the job, and five thousand apiece. Sound good to you, Kirby?'

Red was pushing too hard. Kirby felt

panic grip his gut. There was a lot about Banner that bothered him now. Too many questions to be answered and too little time. Why would a man like Banner choose to hide himself in the mountains? He wasn't the type to hide from anything.

His gaze moved down to the big, black, ivory-gripped Colt resting easily on Banner's hip, eager and deadly. No notches, but that didn't mean anything. A man like Banner wouldn't need reminding of the men he had killed. Something about the gun struck a chord in Kirby's memory ... a black, ivory-gripped Colt? He had heard of one man who favoured a gun like that, but he was dead—his remains resting somewhere in the Lost River country. Still ...

He glanced at Cody as if seeking confirmation of his suspicions. Only regret showed in that world-weary face. It was enough. There was no doubt in Cody's mind about the outcome of the fight. Kirby felt the blood chill in his veins.

He turned abruptly. 'It's time to ride, Red,' he said quietly.

Red stared at his partner. He had never known Kirby to back off from a fight before. 'You scared, Kirby? You letting this jasper buffalo you?' Kirby swore. The kid was a fool. He needed time to talk some sense into him. Too late. Red was already making his move, his hand swooping down towards his gunbutt. Kirby had little choice but to follow the kid's lead. Between them there was an outside chance they could take Banner. It was the only chance they had.

There was no doubt that Banner intended to kill them anyway. Little Paco was his friend and men like Banner didn't take kindly to having their friends threatened.

He heard Red scream as a bullet shattered his elbow. Kirby's gun was in his hand when Banner's slug slammed into his chest and drove him back against the wall. He slid downwards into a sitting position, his legs outstretched. 'You should have warned us, Cody,' he said weakly. 'You should have warned us.'

'I did, Kirby, but you just weren't listening.'

'You could have told us who he was, Cody. Just the real name. That's all I needed to back off. Just the name.'

'It wasn't down to me, Kirby. He would have told you himself, if he had wanted you to know.'

'Damn you, Co ...'

Red stared in horror at his dead partner. Through the pain, nothing Kirby had said made any sense to him, but he would relive this scene in his mind many times before he was through. 'Why don't you kill me, too, Banner? Go ahead. Kill me.'

'I already have, Red. You're going to spend the rest of your miserable life running and hiding from the friends and families of the men you have killed. They'll be coming, Red. News of a crippled gunman travels far and fast. There'll be others, too. Punks like you, quick-trigger artists eager to get another notch on their gunbutts. It won't matter to them that you are a cripple. That will just make it easier for them. The man who kills you will swear blind that there was nothing wrong with your arm—that you were just as fast as you ever were.'

'They'll be coming for you, too, Banner. You did this to me.'

'Nobody here has ever heard of a man called Banner. You made advances to a young *señorita* with a jealous boyfriend. He tried to stop you but you pulled a gun on him. His girlfriend shot you after you took a shot at her boyfriend. No one is going looking for her, Red, but they will be looking for you. You need all the head-start you can get. If you start now you can maybe make it to a doctor in time to save that arm of yours.'

They listened for the sudden rush of hoofbeats in the night as Red left in a hurry. His face grim, Banner moved back into the darkened corner of the room. Paco reached for the whiskey bottle, his face sad. Banner had been forced to kill in defence of his friend. This much Paco knew. Even if Banner had made the men leave, they would have come back and forced Paco or one of the others to take them to Banner's home in the mountains. It was said that Banner had killed many men before coming to live here, and little Paco could well believe it now.

2

Cody hesitated as he looked down at Banner. Maybe he should bide his time in talking to him, but there was no time like the present. And Banner would probably have disappeared again come morning. Besides, he couldn't afford to wait. Banner was his only chance. He steeled himself, glancing down at the whiskey bottle. Paco had felt that the *señor* needed something stronger than beer tonight. Kirby's body had been taken away, but the stench of death still hung strong in the air.

He took a deep breath. He hadn't seen Banner for a long time but there was a change in the man. This man killed too easily for his taste. Still there was no other to take his place. No one to even try. 'Spare a man a last drink before you kill me, too, Banner? That is in your mind, isn't it?'

'I thought about it,' Banner admitted. 'You brought them here, Cody. You knew what would happen.'

'I had no choice, Banner. The major is the man putting up the money. I had to go along with him. Hear me out before you decide to kill me; that's all I ask. Is that too much, Banner?'

The big man pushed the bottle towards him. 'I'll hear you out, Cody, but I won't make any promises.'

Cody filled the glass he had brought from the bar with Banner's whiskey. It looked like good stuff. He stuffed fresh tobacco into his old pipe and lit it before speaking. 'I've been punching cows for the best part of forty years, Banner, foot-loose and fancy free for most of that time. No thoughts for tomorrow or settling down, but time creeps up on a man. All of a sudden he gets to wondering what will happen if he gets hurt bad or gets too old to chase cows for a living.

'It happened to me, Banner, but I got lucky. About twenty years ago I went to work for Tom Craig at Pine Tree ranch. It was like living with my own family—if I had ever known one. I was just a no-account drifter, looking for work when I got into a fight with a couple of drunken Kiowas. They weren't looking for scalps, just a chance to square a few old debts. A couple of days later Tom Craig found me pinned under a dead horse with my leg busted. He took me back to Pine Tree and got a doctor to try and fix up my leg, but I guess it was too late to do much good. I only had a few dollars to my name but that didn't matter to Tom and his family. I was their guest. My days of punching cows were over and that scared me. There was no way I could spend sixteen or eighteen hours a day in the saddle again, but Tom ignored that. He figured my experience was worth something so he made me ramrod.

'It was a hand-out but I took it. For the

first time in my life I felt as if I belonged somewhere. They had a daughter, Tina. She was the prettiest little thing I ever saw in my life. Jade-green eyes and a smile that could melt anyone's heart. She was only about six then but she helped take care of me, bringing my meals, fetching for me, or just sitting and talking to me. I like to think we had a special relationship. She made me realize that my life had never been fulfilled. She was special to me. Still is ... if only in memory.'

He paused, watching Banner roll a cigarette and light it. The big man blew a smoke ring towards the ceiling before speaking. 'You haven't mentioned the girl's mother, Cody.'

'Damn you, Banner. You don't miss much, do you?'

'Sometimes the things we don't say mean the most, Cody.'

Cody tried to keep the pain from his voice when he spoke again. 'Victoria was the most beautiful woman I have ever seen in my life, Banner, but unlike most beautiful women she seemed unaware of it. Her beauty seemed to glow from inside, making her special to everyone who knew her. Tina reflected that beauty. I've done most of the things that a man does, Banner, ridden broncs, chased cows, branded another man's stock, searched for gold. But I found my mother lode at Pine Tree. It was taken from me.'

He hesitated, feeling the pain of memory clutch at his throat. 'Ever hear of something called a Comanche moon, Banner?'

Banner felt the blood drain from his face and a cold shiver run down his spine as his mind travelled back through the dark alley of time. It was a frightening feeling, leaving a man weak and vulnerable. He fought his way back to the present, grateful for the darkness surrounding him. At least, Cody couldn't see the impact his words had had on Banner.

'I've heard,' Banner said quietly. 'Some call it a blood moon. For some reason there's a red mist over the moon and the Comanche go blood-crazy. Nobody knows why they act that way. Probably don't know themselves. But, I guess, it's just some Comanche superstition.'

Cody's voice faltered with the painful memory when he spoke again. 'It happened one night when I was in town. I didn't even notice the moon until I was on my way home to the ranch. I had a bad feeling then, but it was too late. There was nothing left of the ranch when I got back there. No one left alive. A lot of the crew were still in town. Tom had kept his last bullet for Victoria. After that I don't think he minded dying.'

He emptied his glass in one swallow before refilling it. 'I found Tom's body about ten miles from the ranch next morning. He had died hard but I don't think he really felt anything. Killing Victoria had probably drained him of all pain. I brought him back to the ranch and buried him alongside Victoria. There was no sign of Tina, but I never gave up hope. She was alive and out there somewhere. I could feel it. We tried to find her but it was no use. Trying to catch up with a bunch of nomad Comanch' is like trying to grasp smoke in your hand.

''Bout a week ago we got lucky. A horse trader reported seeing a white girl with a bunch of Comanche. Said he wouldn't have noticed her but for those jade-green eyes. He noticed that she was doing something in the sand with her foot. After the Comanche had left he walked across to where she had been standing. There were four words written in the sand. Just four words. "Tell Cody. Pine Tree". That's when he got in touch with me. I showed him this.' He handed Banner a tin-type photograph. 'He said he couldn't be sure because he'd been afraid to pay too much attention to the girl, but there was a strong resemblance.'

Banner studied the picture of Victoria with the light from a match. 'You were right, Cody. She was a very beautiful woman. Spanish?'

'Pure blood. Her father was a don somewhere south of Sonora. He died when Victoria was eight. They lost the ranch a few years later. She was raised by her grandmother in the old traditions. When Victoria married Tom the old lady moved in with them. Her granddaughter had married well, even if Tom could never be a nobleman.'

His voice tightened. 'Tina was about fourteen, I guess, when Major Buckman arrived at Hidalgo and set about impressing the old lady with fine clothes, good manners, and ready cash. She decided then that the major would be the ideal husband for her great granddaughter, and no one was about to argue with Spanish tradition. By the time Tina was fifteen she was already promised in marriage to Buckman. Victoria and Tom hated the idea, but the old lady's word was law. The major didn't mind. Tina was already a very beautiful girl. And marriage would mean he would eventually get his sticky hands on Pine Tree. With his own land and Pine Tree that added up to a lot of country. The ten thousand dollars he's offering you for bringing Tina back is a small price to pay for a ranch that size.'

'How about you, Cody?' Banner asked. 'I can't see you working for someone like Buckman.'

'I don't, Banner. I'm still running Pine Tree with a lot of help from the bank. If some of that loan isn't paid back soon Tina won't have a home to come back to. The bank will claim the land and split it up into sections for sale to the highest bidder. Even the major hasn't got the kind of money it would take to buy a ranch the size of Pine Tree, and he's never going to be satisfied with just a few sections. He wants it all. He's already taken over most of the land surrounding Pine Tree with the help of Jack Stagg, and a couple of other hired guns. Without Tom, there's no one to protect them from Buckman now. I own a few hundred acres of Pine Tree, Banner. Tom willed it to me before he died. It's yours along with Buckman's ten thousand if you agree to help find Tina and bring her back to Pine Tree.'

Banner rolled another cigarette and lit it, before speaking. 'Why me, Cody? I haven't crossed the border in two years, and I no longer hunt Comanches ... unless they come looking for me. But they don't any more.'

'You are the only man who's gone into the Lost River country and come out again alive. Leastways that's what I heard. That's where Tina is, Banner, at Ghost Warrior's stronghold in the Lost River. And you are the only man who can bring her out of there. The only man.'

Banner got to his feet abruptly, his face bleak. 'You ever hear how I got myself into the Lost River stronghold, Cody?'

'Rumours, Banner. I heard rumours.'

'Then you'll know why I won't be going

back,' Banner said, moving towards the door of the cantina.

Once more the deathly moaning of the wind could be heard as he flung the door open wide and strode into the night. Cody's words followed him:

'She needs you, Banner. No one else can help her.'

3

Cody entered the brightly lit saloon, his eyes seeking out and finding the big impressive-looking man seated at one of the poker tables. Major Buckman was always an easy man to spot in any crowd. He made sure of that, Cody thought cynically.

As usual, Jack Stagg hovered near Buckman's shoulder, his mind and body alert for any kind of trouble. The major wasn't a very popular man. Since his arrival at Hidalgo, with the help of Jack Stagg, he had ridden roughshod over anyone who stood in his way. Many small ranches had already fallen prey to the major's ambition. Since Tom's death, that ambition had run unchecked. With Tom, the ranchers had someone to turn to in times of trouble, but Buckman had been playing his cards close to his chest then. Now there was no one to stand between him and the things he wanted. No one to stand between them and a greedy, unscrupulous man.

Cody swore, and elbowed his way through the crowd. It seemed that every cow-pusher in Texas was gathered here in the Palace saloon tonight. It was something else that the major owned and business was good. Grabbing a bottle and glass from the bar, Cody headed for a deserted table in the far corner of the room. He glanced once more at the major before turning his attention to the bottle. Hope had died for him, along with Kirby, in Paco's Cantina last night but maybe he could find that hope again—if he got drunk enough. Sooner or later he would have to face the major, but later was better. He had failed, and he didn't want to admit it, even to himself.

Across the room, Jack Stagg's quick, cruel eyes had noted the arrival of Cody. Leaning forward, he whispered in Buckman's ear. The impulse to touch Buckman's shoulder was aborted. The major didn't like to be touched. That was a lesson that Stagg had learned early.

'Cody just came in alone,' he whispered. 'Looks like he doesn't want any company, right now.'

Buckman frowned as he glanced in the direction of Stagg's stare. Damn, it didn't look good. Where the hell were Kirby and Red? Maybe they were still in Mexico looking for Banner. It made sense. Cody was an old man, subject to the ailments of old age. A man like that could give up on the search but somehow he didn't think so. As long as he was breathing Cody wouldn't give up on his search for Tina. Something was wrong. Where the hell were Kirby and Red?

'We'll talk to him back at the ranch, Stagg. Make sure he gets there, and make sure he's sober. There are a lot of questions I want answered.'

Rain was sweeping in again as the three men approached the dimly lit ranch-house. The major, as usual, rode in his buggy. Important men never rode in the elements. At the sound of hooves in the yard, an old Mexican appeared to lead the horses into shelter. The stable was also his home where he had a small room with a pot-bellied stove at the rear. Stagg held open the door for the major to enter the house first. Buckman liked that. It showed respect and increased his sense of self-importance. With his brandy glass full, he seated himself in his favourite chair near the log fire. The chair fitted his bulk comfortably. Lighting a cigar, he looked at Cody as if noticing him for the first time.

'You've got a report to make, Cody.'

'I'm not in the army, Major, and neither are you—if you ever were. Sometimes I wish I was in the army. At least, I would have a purpose in life then. Right now, I'm just a tired, beaten old man, and I'm getting older every second.'

'You're not making sense, Cody. I sent you out to do a job. You had help, but you came back alone. Why? Where are Kirby and Red?'

'Kirby's dead, and Red's as good as,' Cody answered wryly, enjoying the look on Buckman's face.

'Am I supposed to understand that?'

'You were asking for trouble when you sent Kirby and Red to handle a man like Banner. He had them spotted as a couple of cheap gunslicks the second he saw them. He killed Kirby and crippled Red. That bother you, Major? No, I guess not. There are always plenty of cheap gunmen about.'

He avoided looking at Jack Stagg. Gunmen like Stagg never came cheap. He liked to think of himself as a professional, a specialist in the art of killing, with a special liking for the razor-edged knife he kept between his shoulder-blades. Rumour had it that he had killed his first man at the age of twelve, a drunken cowboy he had found asleep in an alley. The weapon had been a straight-edge razor. There was no reason given for the killing other than Stagg had wanted to find out what it was like to kill a man. It had felt good.

By the age of eighteen, he had discovered that killing could be a profitable as well as a pleasurable business. Now tough men crossed the street when they saw Stagg coming, knowing that the half-breed Yaqui walked the thin line between sanity and madness. Stagg liked to kill his victims slowly, an inheritance from his Yaqui father. That thought was enough to make most men cringe and avoid him. But that reputation served Buckman's purpose.

Cody lit his foul-smelling pipe, dismissing Stagg from his thoughts. He didn't matter. Nothing mattered any more. He turned his attention back to Buckman. 'You got your report, Major. Right now, I'm heading back to the saloon and I'm going to get good and drunk. Probably spend the rest of my life that way. Guess that's the only way I'm going to be able to live with myself.' He paused, taking a deep breath, unwilling to force the words from his tight lips. 'Banner isn't coming. He turned you down.'

Another time he would have felt a deep satisfaction knowing that not everyone danced to Buckman's tune. But now the words hurt—the final execution of hope. His last chance of seeing Tina again had died along with Kirby in that little village with no name.

Banner had turned them down, but that wasn't the Banner he had once known. This man was hard, bitter, with an ingrained toughness. Yet even mention of the Lost River stronghold had seemed to frighten him. Or was it Ghost Warrior's name? It didn't make sense. Banner was born without fear. He had proved that when he faced up to Kirby and Red. Yet ...

Buckman poured himself another drink, his face thoughtful. Cody's plan had failed, and it was the only plan they had. Cody had convinced him that Banner was the only man for the job ... the only white man who stood a chance of getting into and out of the Lost River country alive. But Banner wasn't coming. He had turned down $10,000. Only a fool or a coward would turn down that much money. This wasn't a job for a fool or a coward so maybe they were better off without him.

'What went wrong, Cody? Why wouldn't Banner take the job?'

Cody shrugged. 'Who knows? Banner has his own reasons for doing things. Maybe Kirby and Red rubbed him up the wrong way.'

'That doesn't help. Right now, we have to rethink our whole strategy. We need a new plan, and we need it fast. Any ideas?'

Stagg grinned. 'Who needs Banner? Give me twenty men and I'll ride into Ghost Warrior's camp and wipe them all out. All I have to do is find a Comanche and persuade him to show me the way into the stronghold. He'll be glad to help us. I guarantee it.' He slipped the razor-edged knife from between his shoulder-blades to emphasize his words.

Buckman winced. Stagg's plan was typical of the man himself, crude and savage. But it was the only plan they had. Only the fact that there would be so many men involved bothered him. Above all else he needed the girl to remain anonymous, and it would be hard to keep her identity secret with so many men involved in a raid on the stronghold. Still, at present, there was no other plan in sight. With a little refinement, and Stagg leading the attack, there was an outside chance that he could keep the girl under cover until he brought her back to the ranch.

He glanced at Cody sharply. 'How much does Banner know?'

'Enough; but he won't be talking. He isn't about to do anything to upset your social status, Major.'

Satisfied, Buckman nodded. From what Cody had told him about Banner he didn't sound like a talker. He had told him little enough anyway. Cody had believed his lie of thinking only of the girl.

'How soon can you recruit the men you need, Stagg?'

Jack Stagg shrugged. 'A few days. News of ready money travels fast. I figured on getting them from across the border. We'll head from there to the Lost River. Your name won't be mentioned. No one will ever know they are working for you. It will be a private job. I'll have my own reasons for attacking the stronghold and nobody will be asking me any questions. I'll have the girl back here within a month.'

Buckman smiled, one of his rare smiles. Stagg had more brains than he had given him credit for. All that remained now was for Stagg to find a stray Comanche. That shouldn't prove too difficult. Knowing Stagg's methods, getting that Comanche to show him the way to the stronghold would be easy.

'You can leave first thing in the morning, Stagg. I'll have the money ready for you.'

Stagg smiled. Good. He wouldn't be getting the kind of money that Buckman had offered Banner, but there would be a nice bonus in it for him. And there was also the prospect of getting his hands on a bunch of stinking Comanche. That was good news, and maybe the best part of the job. 'I'll bring back Ghost Warrior's scalp. You can hang it right over your fireplace. Should look real nice there.'

'You got more chance of losing your own scalp,' a strange voice said, from the depths of an armchair in the other room.

4

They watched the tall man stride easily into the main room and stop before Jack Stagg. Cold, steel-grey eyes challenged the half-breed before dismissing him as a threat. He had seen Stagg's type before; men who liked all the odds in their favour before making a move. A slight grin touched his face before moving away, further irking the man.

Major Buckman watched the interplay between the two men with hidden amusement. If this was Banner, and he was pretty sure it was, Cody hadn't lied about his toughness. No one had ever treated Stagg with such contempt before and walked away unscathed. It couldn't last. Stagg would never be able to forget the way Banner had treated him. Even now his hand was stealing towards the knife at the back of his neck.

'Pull that knife, Stagg, and I'll kill you,' Banner said flatly, watching the man's action in a wall mirror.

Stagg's hand froze. There was no doubt that Banner was quick with a gun. Kirby and Red were proof of that. He let his hand fall, making sure it was well away from his gunbutt. No sense in pushing things right now. Banner's time would come when he least expected it.

Buckman let his amusement show now. Stagg had needed to be taken down a peg or two for a long time. The 'breed was used to having men cower before him—but not Banner. Banner would never back down to any man. Stagg had met his match and didn't like it.

He looked up as the tall man parked his hip on the corner of the desk and spoke again. The voice, like the man himself, had an edge to it. 'I'm Banner. Let's talk business. Your men mentioned ten thousand. I'll take half now, the rest when I bring the girl back.'

Buckman smiled. 'You make it sound easy, Banner. If it's that easy maybe I should go myself and save a lot of money.'

'You won't make it,' Banner said coldly. 'Neither will Stagg. Ghost Warrior will have Stagg and his men spotted before they get within ten miles of the stronghold. He'll send out a couple of decoys to lead them into a blind canyon where he'll be waiting with the rest of his boys. Those who survive the ambush will wish they hadn't. I know what the Comanches do to their captives and it isn't pretty.'

'But you can do it while twenty men fail?' Buckman mused. 'What makes you so special, Banner?'

'I've been there, Buckman, and I'm still living. I've been into the Lost River stronghold and come out again. That makes me special. I'm the only white man who can say that. I know every inch of the stronghold, every lookout post, and how to get past them. I'll be up there waiting for the right time to get the girl out. There's also the element of surprise: I'm the last man in the world Ghost Warrior's men will be expecting to see. That gives me a big edge.'

He paused long enough to roll a cigarette and light it. 'You haven't got much time to think about it, Buckman. Winter's moving in and I want to be in the Lost River country before the snow comes.'

Buckman looked confused. Very little of what Banner had said made any sense to him, but the tall man seemed confident of his ability to bring back the girl, and that was all that really mattered. With the girl back at Pine Tree, he would soon become the most powerful man anywhere around here and the richest. Banner's confidence was starting to rub off on him, but he wasn't going to make it too easy for him. Banner had to know who was boss, just as Stagg had had to learn.

'I still think Stagg's plan has a certain merit. With twenty good men, he could ride right through a bunch of deadbeat Comanche with very little trouble. He could wipe out the Comanche threat in one stroke.'

Banner blew smoke towards the ceiling. 'Hear tell of another man who thought he could do the same to the Sioux. His name was Custer and his ego got a lot of good men killed. Take Ghost Warrior for a fool and he'll bury you. He's got fifty, maybe sixty men with him at the stronghold now, and more joining him all the time. He's got a big reputation among the Comanche and it's growing.'

'Sounds as if you admire him, Banner?' Stagg snapped.

Banner looked thoughtful for a moment before his eyes turned bleak. 'I'll kill him first chance I get, but I won't be looking for him. It's just a fact of life that I'll have to kill him some day ... or he'll kill me.'

'I'd like to see that, Banner,' Stagg

grinned. 'Wanna guess who I'll be rooting for?'

Buckman's glance silenced him. There would be plenty of time for words later when he stood over Banner watching him die.

'You could lead Stagg and his men to the stronghold, Banner,' the major said. 'That would shorten the odds quite a lot.'

'I work alone,' Banner stated. 'Twenty men trailing behind me raise a lot of dust and a lot of noise. Besides, it's a good way to get the girl killed. Twenty men riding into a Comanche camp are going to be shooting at anything that moves, that includes women and kids. And it won't make much difference to the kind of trash that Stagg will be hiring. My way, I identify the girl before moving in.'

He was right. There was a good chance of getting the girl killed if Stagg's bunch rode into the stronghold. With her dark skin and hair she would look like any other

Comanche squaw at first glance. And there wouldn't be time for a second. He moved towards the safe, his mind made up. He couldn't take chances with the girl's life. There was too much at stake. There was less in that safe than he would have liked, but this was an investment. He handed the bundle of notes to Banner.

'Five thousand, Banner. That's a lot of money to lose if you don't come back.'

'I will have lost a lot more,' Banner said wryly, stuffing the wad of money into his shirt. 'But I won't be spending it where I'll be.'

Buckman smiled. 'I like you, Banner. You've got brains, and in your own way you are just as ruthless as I am. You are going back to the Lost River country because you have something to prove to yourself. You don't give a damn about the girl or the money, but you will bring the girl back—or die trying.'

He lifted a cigar from the humidor and lit it. 'The girl's been a prisoner of the

Comanche for the best part of ten years. In most people's book that makes her a Comanche, too. She's no longer white. That's part of the reason I created the lie about her. As far as everyone around here is concerned, Tina was at her uncle's ranch south of Sonora the night the Comanche hit Pine Tree. I don't want them to learn any different. Cody went along with the lie. He still does, but he doesn't like it. Cody wanted to plaster the country with reward posters for the girl after she disappeared, but I persuaded him against it, for the girl's sake.'

'You sure it was for the girl's sake?' Banner asked quietly. 'It seems to me that you are a man with big ambitions, Buckman. Being called a squawman wouldn't help those ambitions along, would they?'

Buckman's face tightened. 'You're a smart man, Banner. But my way it works out for the girl and me. Cody saw reason. He doesn't want people pitying her every time they look at her. The women would be the worst. They make most men look gentle by comparison. Every one one of them will be saying that they would rather slit their own throats than let a dirty Comanche near them. Most of them will even believe it. Tina hasn't done that, and they'll never forgive her for it.'

'He's right, Banner,' Cody said quietly. 'There are a lot of females around here would make her life hell if they knew where she had been for the past nine years. She's been through enough, Banner; I don't want her hurt any more.'

Buckman laughed. 'You're wasting your time, Cody. Banner doesn't care about people. He's got his own personal reason for going back to the Lost River country, and it has nothing to do with the girl. The money I'm offering for the girl's return is a bonus. That's all. The girl doesn't mean a thing to him, but he'll bring her back because he wants that extra five thousand. You were wrong about him,

Cody; Banner's just as greedy as the rest of us. Compassion is a human weakness that Banner can't afford in his business. Am I right, Banner?'

'Close enough,' Banner admitted, rolling a smoke. 'But then most of us don't want to face up to the truth about ourselves, do we, Buckman? I stopped off at Pine Tree on my way here. Nice piece of land, big enough for a man to overlook where the girl has been for the past nine years. Problem is, Buckman, I wonder if you are a big enough man to help the girl forget where she's been?'

Buckman's face tightened for an instant. Banner had read him right and he didn't like it. 'So we both get a bonus, Banner. Anything wrong with that?'

Banner shrugged. 'My job is just to get the girl back. What happens after that is none of my business. I'll be leaving first thing in the morning. With a little luck we should be back within a month.'

'You make it sound easy, Banner. Too

damned easy. I'd like to know what I'm getting for my money. If you have a plan, I'd like to hear it.'

'You already did, from Stagg. I ride into the stronghold, pick the girl up and ride out again. If my plan works, we'll have a few days' head-start before Ghost Warrior and his men start out after us. Winter's coming on. Pretty soon Ghost Warrior will have to start raiding in Mexico to get supplies to keep his people fed and warm through the winter. He'll leave some of the old men and a few of the young bucks behind to guard the stronghold.'

'How many men do you reckon he'll be leaving behind?'

'Enough,' Banner said. 'If you are thinking of using Stagg on a raid into the stronghold, forget it. A dozen men can hold that place until Hell freezes over.'

'And you still think you can just ride in there and ride out again with the girl?' Stagg grunted. 'You're crazy, Banner. They are going to kill you.'

A slight smile touched Banner's face as his hand closed on the latch. 'They already have, Stagg.'

The door slammed shut on his words as he strolled into the night.

5

Cody studied Banner as the big man rubbed down the black gelding, his face thoughtful, probably thinking of what lay ahead of him. Going back to the Lost River wouldn't be easy for him. Rain still fell steadily but it was now only a short walk from the stables to the ranch-house. Silence had followed them all the way from Buckman's ranch to Pine Tree, but that was expected. Banner rarely had much to say anyway. The man lived inside himself, his thoughts and emotions private, if he had any real emotions. Maybe some day someone would be able to penetrate the hard shell that the man had built around himself, but Cody doubted it.

'What made you change your mind, Banner? I've never known you change your mind about anything before. And I've never known you do anything just for money.'

'Perhaps Buckman was right, maybe I do have something to prove,' Banner said softly as he continued rubbing down the black, his face tense, his mind back in the Lost River country. There were a lot of bad memories back there and he would soon be forced to relive them all over again.

'How long have we been friends, Cody? Eight—ten years?'

The question caught Cody off guard. 'Friends, Banner? I doubt if we have ever been friends. You never let anyone get that close to you, but there's no man I would trust more. I guess we've known each other about ten years, but I don't know any more about you now than I did then. All anyone knows about you is rumours. It's almost as if you don't really exist. No one has seen or heard of you north of the Rio for the past five years. All the rumours said you were dead, killed in the Lost River country, but

I knew different. I heard the whisper of a big man who liked his own company and lived in the mountains south of the border. The description fitted you. I was content to leave you there, Banner, until I found out that Tina was alive and living in the Lost River stronghold. I had no choice but to come after you.

'You started the rumour yourself, didn't you, Banner? You wanted everyone to believe you were dead.'

'I had my reasons,' Banner answered softly. 'You know about me and the Comanches. I've been pushing my luck hard for a long time. The odds were getting shorter, and they weren't in my favour. Ghost Warrior wants my scalp hanging from his war lance. There will be no mistakes the next time we meet.'

Cody searched Banner's face for fear, but found none. There was doubt though. Banner wasn't sure of the outcome if Ghost Warrior and he did meet again. 'I can understand that, Banner. They say that you are the only man that Ghost Warrior ever feared. And he doesn't scare easy. You gave the Comanche plenty of reason to be afraid of you. They didn't name you Comanche Killer for nothing.'

He glanced at the big knife resting on Banner's left hip. A knife was Jack Stagg's favourite weapon but Banner was said to be a master with it. Stories had been told of Banner entering Comanche camps at dead of night and killing selected braves, the pride of the Comanche fighting force, with that blade. It was the kind of thing that Banner would do without thinking twice.

Despite the fact that the ranch house had been completely rebuilt since the attack, the presence of Victoria and Tom still lived in it. Cody could sense that presence each time he entered. Perhaps they were awaiting the return of Tina? He poured a couple of drinks, passing one to Banner, wondering if the big man had ever known a home? It seemed that

Banner had spent most of his life under the sky. How much did he really know about him? Nothing, except the years had turned him into a cold, emotionless man. Life, his or anyone else's, no longer held any meaning for Banner.

'I still don't know your reason for changing your mind, Banner. Was it because of me?'

Banner shrugged. 'Don't really know, Cody. I had no plans for going anywhere near the stronghold again, but I know how the Comanche treat their captives. That girl is going through all kinds of hell, and it looks like I'm the only one who can help her. Maybe I'm not as dead inside as I thought I was.'

It was a lie and he knew it. Cody would never understand his real reason for going back. It didn't make sense, even to him. Only a fool or a man contemplating suicide would think that way.

White Crow studied the country below

without much interest. The maze of canyons had been part of his life for a long time now. The white men could never find their way through there to the heart of the stronghold, even if they were foolish enough to try. Only one man had ever found his way in; only one man with courage enough to try, but now Banner was dead. White Crow smiled at the thought. Comanche Killer was dead. Now the Comanche could sleep safely in their lodges. Yet, for a long time after news of Banner's death had reached them, the fear had remained. Only when Ghost Warrior had told them himself of seeing Banner's death with his own eyes had the fear ebbed.

High above him the white man eased his muscles as he changed position, slowly and carefully. There was little chance that the lookouts would be watching the rocks above them, but Banner wasn't about to take any chances. One glimpse of him now would blow his entire plan. He would enter the stronghold when the time was right. Already he had spent over a week watching and recognized White Crow in his usual position on the bluff. White Crow had the early morning watch. Good. That meant he would be covering the way out when Banner finally made his move. The old man would recognize Comanche Killer and that was essential to his plan.

The weather was getting colder with the promise of an early start to the winter. The chill was in him, too, but it had little to do with the weather. That chill had been with him ever since he had decided to come back to the stronghold. He could hear the roar of the river far below—the river that had caused him nightmares for a long time. But he was back now, ready to face up to his fears.

The imposing figure of Ghost Warrior emerging from his lodge caught his eye. There was no mistaking him. Soon he would be leading his braves on the raids into Mexico to bring back the food and clothing needed to keep his people fed and warm during the winter. They were already making preparations to leave. Any day now they would set off. They had to get to Mexico, carry out the raids and bring back the supplies before the snow started to fly. He glanced at the sky again, reading the signs there. He had been a part of this country for a long time now and, if his guess was right, they were in for a long, hard winter. He shook his head slowly. It could put a crimp in his plans, too.

As yet, Banner hadn't been able to identify Tina. Her dark hair, so much like all the others, made it difficult. All he could hope for was the girl was still able to recognize her own name. That was the one possibility he hadn't discussed with Cody—the possibility that the girl was no longer sane. It had happened too many times before. A young girl could, and usually did, lose all sense of identity and reality. The fact that the girl had been able to write Cody's name in the dust for the horse trader to see gave him some hope, but a lot could have happened between then and now. He would have to handle things as they came. Every plan had to end somewhere.

6

Banner moved through the false dawn, swiftly and carefully. He wanted to be in position when the time came. The horses were already tethered in a blind canyon near to the stronghold entrance. He steeled himself, it was almost time. Ghost Warrior had left on his Mexico raids two days before. It hadn't been easy but Banner had forced himself to bide his time, needing as many miles as possible between him and Ghost Warrior before going in after the girl. It was a sure bet that one of the braves would be on Ghost Warrior's trail a few minutes after Banner left the stronghold to give him the news of Comanche Killer's return. The news would hit Ghost Warrior hard and he would be coming back fast. Banner needed all the head-start he could get.

He moved back through the early light, heading towards the river and looking down into that raging torrent far below. Lost River. The gateway to Hell! He shuddered as his eyes swept down towards that deep dark hole where the river disappeared into the bowels of the earth. This was medicine country. The Comanche believed that that river led straight to Hell. Only Banner knew the truth.

The mist was rising from that river now, thick and eerie with the dawn. Banner waited, letting the mist settle around his tense body. Everything depended upon the next few minutes. There was always the chance that there was someone in the camp who wouldn't recognize Banner or hadn't heard the legend. If that happened Banner would be dead—but for real this time.

Suddenly there were signs of activity in the camp. Banner waited, silent, as yet unnoticed. It was one of the older men who noticed him first. His eyes widened in terror. No. It could not be. Banner was dead. There were many witnesses to his death. Women screamed and ran back under cover as Banner moved silently forward. A young boy reached for his bow and received a cuff about the ear as Banner came towards them. He let his breath out slowly. So far so good. His plan seemed to be working. The mist moved with him, adding to his spectre-like appearance. He stopped in the centre of the camp, calling the girl's name twice, his voice low. A movement at a lodge entrance caught his eye. There was no doubt that this was the girl he was looking for. There could be no mistaking those lovely, jade-green eyes.

His voice was soft, reassuring. 'Cody sent me. He wants you back home again. Follow me, but not too close in case of trouble. I've got everything you need.'

'Not quite everything,' she said quietly, disappearing back into the lodge. Banner swore. All he needed now was a hesitant woman on his hands. He clenched his fist tightly, hating the thought of hitting a woman, but if that was what it took. The girl reappeared, carrying a young boy. Banner swore again. That was something that he hadn't even considered. It was all he needed to slow him down, an extra passenger, and a kid to boot. He would be hard pressed to keep to his schedule now.

The young woman moved to his side, but not too close as he had instructed and they moved towards the trail leading from the stronghold. Men moved aside as they moved towards them, puzzling Tina. Who was this man that he had such power over Ghost Warrior's men? It didn't make sense. They were afraid of him. She could see the fear in their eyes. But he was taking her back home to Cody. That was all that mattered. Cody had sent him and chosen the right man for the job it seemed. But that was typical of Cody. The thought of seeing him again thrilled her, but it was still a long way ahead. First they had to get out of the stronghold.

She moved closer to the man, needing his strength, but keeping clear of his gunhand. If trouble came the man would need his right hand clear and her out of the way. Still there was no move to prevent them leaving. Whoever the man was he was in complete control of the situation. He could, would, take her back to Pine Tree and Cody. And nothing would ever stop him.

As soon as they were out of sight of the camp, the tall man vanished from her side to return a few minutes later leading two saddle mounts and a pack horse. Reluctantly, he held the boy while she mounted, his face cold and emotionless. There was no doubt that the boy hadn't figured in his plans. How could he? He hadn't even known that the boy existed. If he had known ...? What then, she wondered.

'The boy is my son,' she said flatly.

'Perhaps you think I should leave him behind, Mr ...?'

'Banner,' he answered evenly. 'Makes no difference to me what you do with him, but I know someone who isn't going to be too happy about him. Make up your mind quick. I want to be as far away from here as possible before Ghost Warrior returns.'

Her green eyes blazed angrily at him. Could he be serious? Did he really think she could abandon her own son? What kind of man was he? Banner? The name struck a chord in her memory. Banner. He was the one they called Comanche Killer. A man who hated Comanches with every fibre of his being. The fact that her son was only half-Comanche was enough to kindle that hatred. The fact that he was only a boy wouldn't make any difference to a man like Banner. She would have to be careful. He was even capable of killing a five-year-old boy if that boy was a part-blood Comanche. How could Cody send a man like Banner to bring her back?

73

But then, Cody couldn't have known she had a son, could he? She forced herself to hide her fear as she looked at Banner again. 'Ghost Warrior is in Mexico. He left a few days ago.'

'He'll be heading back as soon as he learns that I've returned,' Banner stated coldly. 'Right now, they are sending someone after him to tell him that I've been in the stronghold. Maybe he'll leave some of his braves behind to carry on with the raids, but I doubt it. Too bad. It looks like a lot of empty bellies this winter.'

'That thought seems to please you, Banner,' she said. 'There are also a lot of women and children in the stronghold.'

'I know. Ghost Warrior will have to do his raiding a little closer to home, and there are a lot of men waiting out here with loaded guns just itching to get a chance at Ghost Warrior and his bunch.'

She watched him swing easily into the saddle, her eyes still blazing with anger. The tall man had risked his life to rescue her, but already she was missing the security of the stronghold, if only for her son's sake.

Snow was falling steadily as they left the maze of canyons behind. He had been right; winter was moving in early. Good. The snow would cover up their tracks and help slow down the pursuit. Even an Apache couldn't read tracks under snow. Of course, having the kid along would slow them down some, but they should still reach Devlin in a little under a week, barring any trouble. Ghost Warrior wouldn't attack a town that size, even if he found out that was where they were heading. They would rest up for a couple of days before going on again, using back trails and keeping under cover.

The woman was keeping her distance, glancing at him fearfully once in a while as she clung tightly to the boy—somehow he couldn't bring himself to think of the boy as her son. He was a Comanche, and that was it. He shrugged it off, checking his back trail. There was no sign of pursuit. Not that he expected any yet, but there was always the chance that one of the young bucks in the stronghold didn't believe the legend of Comanche Killer. The older, wiser heads in the stronghold would tell them there was no way to track a ghost, but Banner's scalp was a prize beyond compare, and there was always some fool who would risk his life to get it.

The land stretched before them as they topped the ridge; white and empty of life or so it seemed. Banner knew differently. Probably a hundred pairs of eyes watched them, some the hunted, others the hunters. It was the way of life, and Banner had been both in this land he knew so well. The land would come to life again after they passed. He urged the black forward, a bad feeling growing in his gut. Only a hunch, but he had long since learned to respect these hunches. Trouble was coming. He could feel it.

They had almost reached the shelf when the trouble came: two men riding towards them from a stand of thick timber. They had been waiting there for them. Nothing was more sure. Using his left hand, Banner unbuttoned his coat, giving him access to his pistol as the distance closed between them. One of the men carried a rifle, cocked and ready before him, and aimed at Banner. The other man, confident of his ability with a short gun, kept his hand on his gunbutt, his coat wide open. They were fanning out now as they closed in, their eyes never leaving Banner. He signalled the girl to move aside out of the line of fire.

Twelve feet separated them when they came to a stop, their grins mocking Banner. 'Looks like we found ourselves a squawman, Smithy,' the heavier of the two men said.

'And a big hunk of money, Mick,' the other man added. 'Guess a big reputation doesn't mean much when someone's got the drop on you. We'll take the girl off your hands, Banner. I guess Ghost Warrior will be satisfied with your body.'

Banner made his move then. There was little chance of him getting off a shot before the man with the rifle, but he had to try, and the man with the carbine would have to be his first target. The best he could hope for was his sudden move would put the rifleman off his aim. His shot almost merged with the rifle shot, and the man was already toppling from his horse when Banner's second bullet killed the other man. He was off the black before the second body hit the snow-covered ground. Satisfied that both men were dead, he turned his attention to gathering up their horses, tying their reins to the black's saddlehorn. The black would stay put and keep the other horses with him.

He glanced up at the sky. No sign of the buzzards yet, but they would come and lead the Comanches here, unless he got the bodies covered up quickly. He dragged the bodies to the dry wash nearby. Pain hit him as he started to push the loose earth and rocks over the bodies, but he ignored it until he had the bodies covered to his satisfaction. Slowly he remounted the black, gathering the reins of the spare horses.

There had to be a change of plan now. He had no other option. Tina wouldn't be back at Pine Tree as soon as expected, but he couldn't help that. Those two men had changed his plans for him. He let his gaze wander to the distant mountain range. Even the thought of going back there pained him, but there was no other choice now. It would be a hard ride, but they would make it. They had to.

The sudden change of direction puzzled her. Where was Banner leading her to? There were no towns, ranches or white people in that long valley. No one for at least a hundred miles in any direction. So why was Banner heading there? The doubts were creeping in. She only had

Banner's word that Cody had sent him. What if he had lied? Perhaps Banner had another reason for being here? And she could guess what that reason was: Banner wasn't finished with killing Comanches yet. There was still another scalp he needed for his collection—the most important one. And he was using her to get it.

Banner was picking up the pace, stopping only once to check their back trail. No sign of pursuit. The snow was getting thicker now, building up into a blizzard, wiping out their tracks as soon as they were made. His face looked ashen. Perhaps the cold weather was starting to get to him, but she doubted it. Banner looked as if he had spent most of his life out of doors, and his reputation confirmed it. They said that Banner had once trailed a band of Comanche for two years until he got his chance at the man he wanted to kill.

Wherever Banner was heading his sense of direction seemed unerring, and he was in a hurry to get there. The boy fell asleep in her arms as they travelled into the night. There had been no stops along the way. Dawn was breaking as they reached the narrow pass. Already snow was piling up in that pass, threatening to cut it off before long. As they had travelled they had passed close to the remains of a house, the blackened timbers pointed at the night sky, and she had wondered about it, but resisted comment. Banner wasn't an easy man to talk to anyway.

She hadn't even known that pass was there, and doubted if anyone else did until Banner led them through the winding pass. Somewhere in the distant past Banner must have discovered it by accident. It had to be that way. Where it led to she didn't know. Only Banner knew the answer to that. The snow was beginning to pile up against the outcrop. Within a few hours no one would be able to follow them here, even if they knew about it.

He eased the black to a halt. 'Only one way in and one way out. We're safe now.'

'Are you sure that's what you want, Mr Banner? I thought the idea was to have Ghost Warrior follow us here. We had a chance to head for Devlin but that didn't fit in with your plan, did it?'

'We wouldn't have made it,' Banner said quietly.

'I think we would have, Mr Banner. We would have been safe in Devlin. Ghost Warrior doesn't have enough men to attack a town. You want him to come here. And you'll be waiting for him. He can't get to you in here, but you can get to him with that rifle of yours. You have a big reputation with a rifle. There is probably a place already picked out up here that will give you a good clear shot at Ghost Warrior when he rides into that valley behind us. They won't know where the shot came from and they won't be able to reach us up here. It's a good plan, Mr Banner.'

'Ghost Warrior won't be coming here. After he loses our trail, he'll look around for a while before heading back to the stronghold. Probably pick up another white woman to take your place so one of his braves won't be cold this winter. There are always plenty of white women about, and he'll know where to find them.'

'He won't settle for anyone else, Banner. Ghost Warrior will spend the whole winter out there if needs be. Nothing is going to stop him until he catches up with us, and you know it. I don't like the idea of you using my son and me as bait, Banner, but there's no doubt that your plan will work.'

'Someday I'm going to find out what you are talking about,' Banner said flatly, 'but I ain't got time right now.'

'Are you trying to tell me, Mr Banner, that you don't know that I am Ghost Warrior's wife and this is his son? His only son.'

7

Banner swore silently. The girl's confession that she was Ghost Warrior's wife had hit him hard, harder than he cared to admit. It meant big trouble. Every Comanche for miles around would be on the lookout for them now, and Ghost Warrior would never rest until his wife and son were safe back in his lodge, and Banner's scalp hanging from his war lance. Even if he got the girl back home it would only be a matter of time until Ghost Warrior turned up there, too.

Well, that was someone else's problem. His job was to get the girl back to Pine Tree. After that, Banner would disappear again ... if he got that far. The pain hit him again. Maybe this was as far as he was going to get? Already he could feel himself growing weaker.

The well-built cabin at the top of the narrow trail surprised her. She had no idea that she would find anything like that up here. There was another building too, a stable. Both buildings showed the same care in construction. Obviously whoever had built this place had meant it to last. She dismounted and watched Banner leading the horses towards the stable, his movements slow and laboured. She had been wrong about him.

He hadn't known that she was Ghost Warrior's wife. She was sure of it. If he had known, she had the feeling that she wouldn't be here with him now.

The cabin was surprisingly clean and tidy. Someone had been here recently. But who? And where were they now? His voice startled her. She hadn't heard him come in. 'Jose stays up here in the summer, grazes his goats and cuts hay ready for the winter. My stock is taken care of by his son Pedro in the valley beyond here. Pedro has his own place in the valley, only comes up here in the summer.'

'Where is Jose now?'

'Back in Mexico with his family. The winters up here are too cold for them. They got caught up here a few years back. They've learned to keep the place well stocked up since then.'

He stopped talking then as a sudden shiver ran through his body. Cold. Too damned cold. He knelt to set light to the kindling already laid in the big fireplace, feeling the blood drain from his face. The match flame danced before his eyes, and he felt suddenly weak, drained of all strength. Tina watched in horror as he suddenly pitched forward, unconscious. She rushed forward, dragging him away from the fireplace, gasping in fear as his heavy coat popped open and she gazed at his blood-soaked shirt. So much blood. Could a man lose so much blood and survive? Luckily, he seemed to have stopped bleeding. But what had happened to Banner? Her confused brain searched for an answer. She had it then. The two men! That had to be it. The man with the rifle must have shot Banner before he died. Little wonder there had been a change in plan. Banner wouldn't have made it to Devlin with a bullet in him. He had been lucky to make it this far. The big man hadn't even given an indication that he had been wounded.

She added more wood to the fire before beginning her search for things she could use as medical supplies. She was in luck. Jose had planned ahead, a cupboard yielded everything she would need. She set the water on to boil. Her face anxious, she set to work on Banner. The bullet had been deflected by the big man's shoulder blade and come to a stop just under the skin below. It would have to come out, if she could bring herself to do it. She had no choice. She found a small thin-bladed knife and sterilized it, steeling herself to cut that bullet out, hoping she wouldn't start it bleeding again. Banner couldn't afford to lose any more blood.

That angry water far below beckoned to him. He looked down into that raging torrent, attracted yet repulsed by that dark swirling water. The black hole called to him, like a siren's song. He moved along the rim drawn to that big black hole and the disappearing river. He was afraid. For the first time in his life he felt fear for himself and didn't like it. Banner was afraid. Banner, the man without fear. A cold sweat soaked his body as he looked again at that black hole. Ghost Warrior stood astride it now, smiling at Banner, calling to him. He stepped back from the rim, but could still hear Ghost Warrior calling to him. In vain, he tried to stop himself running back towards the rim. Banner could hear himself screaming as he launched himself off the rim down into the dark raging torrent below.

Comanche Killer was dead. Every Comanche in Texas knew that. They sang songs about Banner's death. So why were the Comanche after him? Ghost Warrior would be coming after him. But why? What would make Banner so important to Ghost Warrior now? Why now? Banner was safe in Mexico, hidden in the mountains. There had to be a reason why Ghost Warrior would suddenly want to kill him again. But he couldn't remember why.

'Don't move,' the voice was stern yet gentle, and the woman came into his view followed closely by a young boy. Who were they? Even to his, as yet unfocused, eyes she was beautiful. 'Stay where you are, Mr Banner.'

He remembered then. Everything; including why Ghost Warrior wouldn't give up until Banner's scalp was hanging from his war lance.

'There are a lot of things to be done,' he said weakly.

'Everything that needs to be done, has been, Mr Banner. You need a lot of rest before you will be of any use to us again.

You have been unconscious for the past four days. I've made beef stew. Jose left us plenty of provisions so we have nothing to worry about, and the horses have been taken care of. All we need now is for you to get your strength back. Are you ready to eat now?'

'I could do with some coffee,' he said.

'Later.' Her smile seemed to light up the room. 'Coffee was the first thing I wanted when we got here. I don't think that coffee will ever taste as good again as that first cup.'

She brought the first bowl of soup to him, helping support him as she spoon-fed him, knowing he hated being treated that way, but Banner was weaker than he had at first thought. Four bowls of that soup disappeared inside the big man, and already she could feel some of the strength flowing back into his body. Only after the last bowl was finished did she grant Banner's wish for coffee. He managed two cups before sinking back on to the mattress. A few more days and Banner would be back on his feet again for a little while; but not before then, she wouldn't allow it. Tough as Banner was, there was no man on earth tougher than a woman with her mind set on something. She hoped he had sense enough to realize that.

The boy was watching the big man wide-eyed, but Banner wasn't taking any notice of him. In fact, he had barely glanced at the boy since rescuing them from the stronghold. It was as if in Banner's mind he didn't exist.

He was nothing; just another Comanche, albeit a half-breed, to be destroyed like all the others when the time came. The fact that he was Ghost Warrior's son would only add to Banner's pleasure when it came to killing him. They didn't call Banner Comanche Killer for nothing. That he was only a boy wouldn't even occur to a man like Banner.

The thought made her feel sick. Perhaps

she should have let Banner die when she had had the chance, but knew she couldn't do anything like that. Still she would have to watch Banner carefully. There was a lot of hate for the Comanche, and especially Ghost Warrior. The death of his son would hurt him more than any of Banner's bullets. It would also ensure that Ghost Warrior would come after Banner and, no doubt, find him waiting. She pulled the boy closer to her, noticing that Banner was aware of the action and her reason for doing so.

Still feeling weak, Banner opened his eyes. The room was dark but not too far off dawn. Time to test his strength; the girl had been his crutch for too long. It was time to test his strength now without help. The girl had been doing a good job on her own, but it was time to start pulling his own weight. Slowly he eased his legs off his bed and sat up.

Pulling his pants on drained him and made him feel dizzy. He rested until the feeling passed before rising slowly to his feet. The room seemed to spin but he refused to sit back down again. The armchair near the fire seemed a long way off, but he moved forward slowly. Sweat was pouring from him when he finally flopped into that chair. He rested, angry with himself for his weakness. The coffee made him feel better.

Suddenly he was aware of angry jade-green eyes looking at him.

'You don't take orders very well, do you, Mr Banner?'

'Never have,' he admitted quietly.

'I told you not to try and get out of that bed for another two days, didn't I? You are in my power now, Mr Banner, and you don't like it, do you? Ghost Warrior's wife and son are taking care of Comanche Killer and he has to obey orders because he's too weak to do anything else. I've heard of you. No one spends much time among the Comanche without hearing stories of Comanche Killer, how no one is safe from you. There are even stories about you creeping into Comanche camps at night and killing men. Tell me, Mr Banner, is it just Comanche that you have this big hate for, or will any Indian do?'

'Comanche are my first choice,' he admitted flatly. 'But if there's none around ...' He left the rest unfinished. There was no need for any further words.

His answer chilled her, but she still faced him defiantly. 'My son is half Comanche, Banner. Does that make a difference to you?'

'It makes a difference,' he said. 'That and the fact that he's Ghost Warrior's son. I've spent the best part of twenty years hunting down Comanche. I got tired but the hate never died. Sooner or later, I would have had to come looking for Ghost Warrior again. This way is better. Now he'll come looking for me, and I won't be hard to find when the time is right.'

'Are you going to kill his son too, Mr Banner?'

He shrugged. 'In time I guess I will ... unless some Comanche gets me first.'

She shook her head. 'You are a sad man, Banner, a very sad man. Even a five-year-old boy is a victim of your hatred. At least when Ghost Warrior spoke of you there was respect in his voice. Comanche Killer was a great warrior, without fear. There is good and bad among all people, regardless of the colour of their skin. But it is a lot easier to hate someone than to try and understand them. Hating comes easy to you, doesn't it, Banner?'

He ignored her as he rolled a cigarette. Reaching forward to get a light from the fire made him feel dizzy again, but he fought against it. The woman asked too many questions, but there was little chance of her getting any answers from him. It was none of her business. His job was to get her back to Pine Tree. As far as he was concerned, that was the full extent of his involvement with her and the boy. One thing was sure: the major would not take too kindly to having the boy brought back to Pine Tree. The boy would blow his plan wide open. With the kid around, there would be no chance of keeping Tina's past a secret. For sure, she wasn't about to deny her own son, for Buckman's sake or anyone else's. He pitied anyone who tried to persuade her to part with her son. She had to have a certain kind of courage to survive in a Comanche camp. She must have gone through all kinds of hell before Ghost Warrior chose her as his wife.

Well, that was the major's problem, not his. Truth was, Banner wouldn't have liked the idea much either, so he could hardly blame Buckman for the way he would feel when he saw the boy. Maybe they were a lot alike, after all. Him and Buckman. The thought disturbed him but he shrugged the thought aside. That was one problem he would never have to face up to. He wondered how Buckman would handle it? He knew that Tina having a half-breed son wouldn't make any difference to Cody.

She still watched him, knowing she wasn't going to get answers to her questions. Banner wasn't the type to ask or answer questions, unless he felt the need to. He had been alone too long, and no longer felt the need to talk. But somehow she had to get to the man inside. It was the only way she would ever feel safe with him—if only for the boy's sake. Perhaps Banner could forget that she had been living as a Comanche squaw but he could never forget that the boy was a half-breed Comanche and the son of Ghost Warrior.

She tried again. Perhaps if she could get Banner talking, establish some sort of communication between them. 'There is one thing that puzzles me, Banner. You were able to walk into the stronghold and out again without a shot being fired. Why didn't they try to kill you? Why were they afraid of you?'

'No point in trying to kill me: I'm already dead. Didn't they tell you that

I was once a prisoner in the stronghold, too?'

'I think they were afraid to,' she said quietly. 'Banner's name was spoken only in whispers.'

He felt his mind slip back through the dark passages of time. When did it happen? Five years ago? He couldn't be sure. Time had little meaning for Banner. It seemed that most of his life had been spent hunting and killing Comanches. A wasted life to most men, but not Banner. It was the life that he had chosen or had been chosen for him. His luck had run out the day he had been caught out in the open by Ghost Warrior's band. It was only a matter of time. It had taken a couple of days, but Ghost Warrior had bided his time, sending men in to tempt Banner until he had run out of ammunition. There had been a smile on Ghost Warrior's face as Banner stood there with only his Bowie knife for defence as thirty Comanche closed in on him on horseback. A war club scrambled his senses and he had been taken captive.

It would have been easy for them to kill him then but that wasn't Ghost Warrior's plan. He would put Banner on display in the stronghold. Banner had been a thorn in his side for too long, his name spoken in hushed whispers among even the bravest of his men. It was said that almost a hundred warriors had died at his hands. But no more men would die at the hands of Comanche Killer. Banner's reign of terror had ended. Ghost Warrior was now the greatest of all the Comanche; Banner's capture was proof of it. Many other Comanche would now join up with Ghost Warrior. He would be the chosen one to lead them in the fight against the white men. They would take Banner to the Lost River stronghold. There was no escape from there. When the time was right, Banner would die slowly to prove how strong he was. A weak man would die quickly, without respect, as was the Comanche way. But Banner would die slowly as befitting a powerful enemy.

Banner had been trying to get into the Lost River stronghold for a long time but had failed. Now, his plan was to get out of there, he thought wryly. Every rock, every stunted tree was etched into his memory as they led him to the stronghold. There was no need to blindfold him. No one had ever escaped. Besides, there were guards all over. No one could even approach the place without being seen. There was only one way out but only a crazy man would even consider it. Still, Banner found himself drawn to the rimrock, staring down into that big black hole. Maybe the Comanche were right. Maybe that river did run straight to the bowels of Hell. There was something about that raging torrent and big black hole that wouldn't sit right with any man, red or white.

There never was any real choice anyway, he thought bitterly. Sooner or later he would have to make that jump and take his chances with the river. Sooner was better. Each day he was getting weaker. The constant beatings from the squaws with the thin willow sticks they carried was beginning to get to him, sapping his strength. Soon he would be too weak to even fight with the dogs for the scraps of food thrown to them. That was a spectacle the Comanche enjoyed—the great Comanche Killer fighting dogs for scraps.

Ghost Warrior's fame had spread, his band grew. Men came to view Comanche Killer and stayed. Any man who could capture the great Banner had to be the finest warrior of them all with the strongest medicine.

He would be the man to follow, the man who would lead them to victory over the hated white men.

It was time. He had no choice now. Soon he would be too weak to even think about it. The river wasn't flowing as fast as usual. A dry spell. Early morning. Nothing between him and the rimrock. He picked his spot carefully, aiming at what he thought would be the deepest part of the river. He hoped he guessed right, if not ... hell, it was only a matter of time before they killed him anyway. He heard someone yell as he started his run. Too bad he couldn't take another Comanche with him.

The sudden plunge into the cold water took his breath away. He fought his way back to the surface. Too soon he was being dragged into that dark hole. His body plunged downwards. The fall seemed endless. He couldn't remember much after that.

When he again regained his senses, he was lying in a goatherder's shack with a little Mexican standing over him. The road to recovery was a long hard one. Six months before he was on his feet again. Jose was spending most of his time with him now. There was little else to do. Everything they owned had been sold to pay the gringo doctor for taking care of Banner. But Jose didn't mind. It was a small price to pay for a man's life. Still, he missed his sheep and goats.

Then one day Banner disappeared. He returned a few days later aboard a big black horse and leading a couple of burros. He had paused before Jose, his face, as usual stern. Banner never smiled. 'There are a herd of sheep and goats on the way here. They are the best I could find. I took your son with me to pick them out. He's a better judge than I am of sheep and goats. Bought you a good dog, too.'

He paused, looking into the distance. 'I've got a place across the border. Thought about running some cows there. Think cows, sheep and goats can get along together?'

Jose nodded. Banner did not think as most cowboys did. 'I have seen it done, *señor*. I myself once had a few cows who grazed with my sheep and goats.'

Banner dismounted. 'Your son will be along soon. I'll lead you to my place. We'll travel by night. It's Comanche country.'

He caught the look of alarm in Jose's face. 'The Comanche don't know about my valley. You'll be safe there. You'll have a place to live and plenty of good grazing.'

'You are too generous, *señor*. I cannot accept.'

'I owe you, Jose. I don't like owing anyone. This makes us even. I won't be staying up there with you. Just one more thing, the pass gets blocked in the winter. You may get caught out so always make sure there's plenty of grub up there.'

Jose mumbled his half-hearted protests. The *señor* was too generous. But it was no use. The big man had spoken. He had left soon after. Jose had the feeling that Banner was more comfortable alone; that for some reason he had no desire to get involved with people ever again.

Tina waited silently until Banner finished his story. She had been expecting Bobby when Banner had been a prisoner in the stronghold. She had been too near her time to make the journey to the stronghold and been left at the summer camp. She watched Banner now. There was still a lot left unsaid, a part of Banner that would forever remain hidden.

'You were taking a chance on coming into the stronghold after me. Someone could have taken a shot at you.'

'It was a chance I had to take. I waited until Ghost Warrior left the stronghold before going in. I knew he would be taking the young braves with him. He always leaves the old men behind on guard. The old ones would remember Banner. Banner was the man who jumped into the Lost River. Only immortals survived the river of death. To shoot at an immortal would offend the gods and bring eternal bad luck to the Comanche.'

'Do you think that will stop Ghost Warrior?' she asked quietly.

He shock his head. 'Not him. He captured Banner once. He'll come after me again, and he won't rest until he finds me. There will be no mistakes this time. He'll kill me where I stand rather than risk me escaping again. It will be him or me and no way to avoid it.'

'Do you want to?' she asked softly.

8

Tina watched Banner ease his left arm into his shirt. No sign of pain on the big man's face. Good. That meant the wound was healing. The boy was watching him too but, as usual, Banner was taking no notice. It was as if for him the boy didn't exist. He hadn't even asked his name.

'His name is Bobby,' she said suddenly, 'in case you were wondering.'

'I wasn't,' Banner said, as he moved to the window. Snowing again, or maybe it hadn't stopped yet. Either way, it was good. Even Ghost Warrior wouldn't waste time trying to track them in weather like this. He turned back to pour himself a cup of coffee. As usual, the boy followed him around, seating himself at Banner's side when the big man sat on the bunk again.

For some reason the child had taken an instant liking to Banner, despite the fact that the tall man chose to ignore him.

He was watching him now with his usual cautious eyes. As yet fear and shyness had kept the boy from saying anything to the big man but it didn't stop him dogging Banner's footsteps or trying to imitate him. That Banner didn't like him was obvious, even to a kid. But why? He had given Banner no reason not to like him.

Banner eased his arm into his coat sleeve. The girl had done a good job of fixing him up. She was a good cook too, he admitted reluctantly. Too damn good. A man could find himself getting used to female cooking. But not this man.

It had stopped snowing when he went outside, but it still lay thick on the ground with the signs of more to come. The horses had been well-cared for. Another point in the girl's favour. She had all the makings of a good wife. Too bad it would be the major's. She deserved better—a lot better. Still, it was none of his business. He had been paid to do a job and he would see it through. What happened after that had nothing to do with him. He patted the black, and made friends with the two spare horses. Who knew when he might need them? He fed the horses before going back to the house. The girl was waiting for him with a fresh mug of coffee, the boy fast asleep on Banner's bed. Banner thanked her with a nod before shrugging off his coat. The coffee was good, just the thing to get a man's blood flowing again on a cold day. There was something on the girl's mind, and he had the feeling that he wouldn't like it. He avoided her eyes as he sipped at his coffee.

'How can a man live with so much hate?' she asked suddenly.

He ignored her question as he rolled a cigarette, but she persisted.

'Does your hate extend to five-year-old boys too, Mr Banner ... if they just happen to have Comanche blood in them? It happens that Comanche blood is the same colour as anyone else's. But you know that already, don't you? You have spilled enough of it, haven't you?'

'Not yet,' he answered quietly. He rose to his feet, towering above her. 'It's going to be a long, hard winter, and we'll be spending a lot of time together before we get out of here. It will make it a lot easier if we don't mention Comanches. I don't kill women or kids and that's all you really care about, isn't it?'

She had to admit that it was, to herself anyway, but there were still other questions to be asked. 'How much is the major paying you to bring me back? I can't believe you are doing this for Cody's sake or mine.'

'Ten thousand dollars,' he answered easily.

The reply seemed to please her. 'At least the major values human life more highly than you do.'

'That's something you will have to find out for yourself.'

'Am I supposed to understand that, Mr Banner?'

He shrugged. 'Not sure that I do either.'

Banner moved to the fire and poured himself another cup of coffee, keeping his mind blank. His job ended when he got the girl and boy back to Pine Tree. After that ..., that he would tangle with Jack Stagg was inevitable, but he would handle that when the time came. Until then he had another fight on his hands and that was not to get involved with the girl or the kid.

Tina watched Banner light his cigarette with a twig from the fire. Despite Banner's reputation she now believed that he would protect her and Bobby with the last breath in his body. For the first time since being kidnapped from Pine Tree she felt secure. Banner would stand between them and whatever happened. Cody had chosen the right man for the job. Only now could she understand the fear and awe the Comanche held for Banner. The big man had an inner strength that made most men look weak, even a man like Ghost Warrior.

Slightly hesitant, she asked: 'I can't keep on calling you Mr Banner. You do have a first name, don't you?'

'Matthew ... Matt, but it's been a long time since anyone called me that,' he answered, handing her a cup of coffee.

'Matthew. A Biblical name. Somehow ...'

'Somehow it doesn't fit?' he asked quietly. 'My parents didn't know how I was going to turn out when they named me,' he said, with something resembling a smile. That surprised her. Maybe Banner had some human qualities, after all. She would have to wait and see.

'How did you know about this place?' she asked.

'The cabin? I helped my father build it. He built to last and took a lot of pride in his work. He died before it was finished. I carried on with the work but couldn't live up to the standards he set. After the work was finished, I rode away. I haven't set foot in the cabin since until I came here with you. I found the pass by accident when I was a kid, and the valley beyond here. It's a good place. Even the Indians don't know it exists. I have close on two thousand head of cattle back there in the valley and Jose's son to take care of them through the winter. He's a good hand with cows, but he doesn't share his father's love of sheep and goats. I'll show you the valley when the weather eases up a little.'

It had been a long time since Banner had strung so many words together, she thought. But he still hadn't answered many questions. Instead he had posed another: why hadn't he come back here until now? She still didn't know much about him. And had the feeling that she never would. The man had an ingrained distrust of people and liked it that way.

She looked at him carefully. He still looked ill, his face grey. Working with the horses had sapped his strength. She was angry with him. 'You tried to do too much. Get some rest and don't even think about disobeying me.'

He glanced at the boy sleeping on his bed.

'You can use Bobby's bed. In my room.'

He shrugged and moved into the other room, not noticing the smile on her face. She was probably the only person in the world who could give Banner orders and have him obey so meekly. Ghost Warrior would never believe it.

She was right. He was weaker than he thought. Fully clothed he laid down on the boy's bed, feeling sleep creep over him already. With sleep the memories came flooding back, the diary of a wasted life. Hate had been the only real emotion he had known for the past twenty years, and in the end hate could be the very thing to destroy him. Could a man be stronger than his own emotions? He didn't know. Maybe emotions were the enemy within, the enemies he could never defeat.

There was another enemy that he couldn't avoid: Ghost Warrior. Banner had invaded his stronghold and taken his wife and son. No man could forget or forgive that. Banner must die if Ghost Warrior was to be once again the invincible one.

9

Tina glanced up from her cooking as the big man came into the cabin carrying an armful of wood. He kicked the door shut behind him. There was already enough wood chopped and stowed to last two winters but Banner seemed determined to regain his lost strength as quickly as possible. She had watched him out there for a long time, swinging that heavy axe easily, the blade biting deep into the wood, his face telling her that his thoughts were elsewhere, yet that quick alertness as something, probably a rabbit, moved in the nearby stand of timber. Satisfied, he resumed his work, and again she wondered what thoughts were going through his head.

Strangely, the urge to get back to Pine

Tree had diminished, yet the urge to see Cody again was still as strong. They were safe here. Ghost Warrior didn't know of this place, but he knew her home and would be waiting for her to get back there. Would there be enough men at Pine Tree to defend it against a full-scale Comanche attack? She doubted it. And she would no longer have Banner to protect her and Bobby. When his job was finished he would once more disappear and she would be alone again. The thought frightened her and it showed.

He poured coffee into a cup and handed it to her. 'No sense in getting frightened of something until you come face to face with it,' he said.

'I'm not afraid for myself. I've lived among the Comanche before. I can do it again if I have to, but you know what will happen when Ghost Warrior comes after me at Pine Tree. There won't be a man left alive, and I'll be responsible. Perhaps it would be best if you left me to make my own way back to the stronghold. Ghost Warrior will have scouts all over the country looking for Bobby and me. They'll find us and take us back to him. At least, no one will have to die because of me.'

He faced her, his eyes bleak. 'Ghost Warrior needs about as much of an excuse to kill white men as I need to kill Comanche. The men at Pine Tree will know what to expect when I take you back there. This time Ghost Warrior will find them ready and waiting for him.'

She looked doubtful. 'You know how many men Ghost Warrior has? Over three times as many as the crew of Pine Tree. I've been through one massacre at Pine Tree, I don't want to be responsible for another.'

'You won't be,' he said quietly. 'Buckman has enough men to back up Cody, if it comes down to it. He has to protect his investment.'

She wondered what he meant. 'You don't like Major Buckman, do you? Why?'

He shrugged. 'Maybe he reminds me too much of me. But I only met the man once so I could be wrong.'

'You seem to like his money, Mr Banner?' she said coldly.

'I had a use for it,' he admitted slowly.

She bit her lip. She had promised herself that she wouldn't argue with Banner again. After all, he had risked his life to rescue her, and being well aware of how the Comanche treated their captives that had taken a lot of courage on Banner's behalf. There would have been no more mistakes had he once again fallen into Comanche hands. His death would have been very slow and very painful.

'I'm sorry,' she said suddenly. 'It's just that, with all this land and everything, I didn't think money was that important to you.'

'It was, at the time,' he answered.

She hesitated, trying to find the right words. 'I'd feel safer if you were to stay around Pine Tree for a while after we get back. Cody's a good man, but no one seems to know Indians the way you do, especially Comanches.'

'I'll be around,' he assured her quietly. 'There's something I have to find out for myself before I can ride away.'

Again she wondered what he meant. Sometimes it seemed that Banner was really talking to himself, trying to find the answers to his own questions. Still he had promised to stay at Pine Tree until the Comanche threat had passed. That was enough. Perhaps, in time, she would even get a chance to know the real Matt Banner. The man had depths as yet unreached, she was sure of it. Would anyone reach the real Matthew Banner? She doubted it. Men like Banner were a challenge to any woman. He had compared himself to Major Buckman, but somehow she couldn't. Years had passed since she had last seen that large impressive-looking man, yet he now seemed pallid when compared to Banner. Banner's strength was more than just physical, it was something that he offered to others to feed off, something Buckman would never do. Even as a child her impression of Buckman had been that of a selfish man.

Her eyes had never left Banner as the thoughts circled in her head. He looked tired. 'First you eat, then you rest.'

He seemed about to argue, but she cut in quickly, 'You've been too long on your own, Banner. Most men learned long ago that it doesn't pay to argue with a woman. We never lose, even when we are wrong.'

Again, a half-smile touched his lips. 'You could try asking me instead of telling me,' he suggested.

She smiled. 'I like giving orders. I never had much chance in the stronghold. Besides it's the only chance I'll have of telling you what to do until we leave this place. You'll be giving the orders then and I'll be obeying them. Until then, you will do as I say.'

She spooned beef stew on to his plate.

He could already smell the apple pie baking in the oven, and was eager to get at it. She had found the apples in a barrel. It seemed that Jose had also developed a taste for apple pie. Apple pie had never featured in the stronghold but Bobby found himself liking the smell, too. As usual, Bobby seated himself close to Banner and was rewarded with a slight smile. At last the big man had acknowledged him. He felt pleased and proud. It seemed that he had finally found a friend. Even his mother seemed surprised. Maybe there was hope for Banner, after all.

Banner awakened suddenly, aware that he was no longer alone in his bed. It was late afternoon. His strength was returning quickly and soon there would no longer be any need for the naps after a morning's strength-sapping work. Tina was watching him from across the room, a curious look in her lovely eyes as she wondered what Banner would think about sharing his bed with Ghost Warrior's son. He climbed out of bed quietly, careful not to disturb the boy.

'I went outside, and when I came back he was on the bed with you,' she explained.

He said nothing as he moved towards the fire, his face blank. The kid was starting to get to him and he didn't like it. A life without involvement of any kind was a lot easier. Even spending this much time with Tina and the kid was making him restless. He needed to be on his own again, once more his own man with no one to care for or care about.

As far back as he cared to remember his way of life was to avoid people, and he liked it that way. Still he had the gut-wrenching feeling that life wouldn't be the same for him after this. After his job was done he would have to remould his whole life ... if he could.

The kid was at his side, looking up at him with those big, curious, still sleepy eyes. He had never seen anyone like

Banner before. Even the big Colt, ever-present on Banner's hip was a frightening thing—ever since he had seen the speed with which Banner had handled it when it spat death at the two men on the trail.

Everything about Banner was awesome, the boy's feelings hovering between love and fear. So much about Banner frightened him, yet he felt that he had no real reason to be afraid of the big stern-faced man. Banner wouldn't hurt him; he was sure of it. As yet, the tall man had barely acknowledged him, let alone spoken to him, but he was starting to thaw. Bobby could sense it.

He followed closely as Banner moved towards the door, reaching his heavy coat down from its peg. Quickly, Bobby grabbed his own coat. Tina's eyes questioned Banner as he shrugged into his coat. Perhaps Banner wouldn't want Bobby out there with him? There were times when Banner needed to be alone. She could sense it in him. He nodded and she helped Bobby on with his coat. Snow was falling as Banner stepped out and stood looking into the distance, a faraway look in his eyes.

From the window, Tina watched him, wondering what he was thinking. It was hard to tell with someone like him. Not that there were too many people like Banner about. Bobby stood a short distance away piling up snow. She could hardly believe her eyes when Banner stooped suddenly, scooped up a handful of snow and lobbed it at Bobby. His aim was good. Bobby straightened wondering where the snow had come from. Banner was once again looking into the distance, his face innocent. Bobby went back to piling up snow before another snowball caught him. He looked at Banner again, and caught a glimpse of his mother laughing in the window, and pointing towards Matt Banner. Within seconds, a full scale snow fight was in progress. Banner deliberately missing with his loose-packed missiles. Over a half-hour passed before they finally appeared in the cabin door-way, covered in snow.

'We had a snow fight,' Bobby explained. 'I won.'

'Only because you are smaller than me and harder to hit,' Banner said.

'I'd suggest you get rid of most of that snow off your clothes before you come in here,' Tina laughed. 'Or you'll have another fight on your hands. And no food.'

Banner grabbed the boy by the back of his coat, lifting him back outside quickly. 'You should have warned me about your mother, Bobby. I didn't know she could be so mean.'

'Women are like that,' Bobby explained.

'That a fact? Looks like I've got a lot to learn about them. You'll have to teach me. Never had much to do with them myself. Always been afraid of them. No sense in looking for trouble, I always thought.'

Bobby laughed. 'I'll learn you.'

Banner smiled, as he brushed Bobby

down. 'Looks like it's safe for you to go back in there now, but how about me? You're too small to brush me down and I can't wait out here until you grow up enough to reach me.'

Bobby laughed. 'Maybe I'll have your share of the food, too.' He ducked inside, still laughing.

Banner followed a few minutes later, grinning as he seated himself next to Bobby. Already Tina could sense a new atmosphere in the cabin, a warm, happy feeling—a glow almost. The kind of feeling that she had once known at Pine Tree, and feared she would never know again. A handful of snow had made all the difference.

He was looking at her now. 'He's a bright kid,' he said. 'I guess you can start making plans for him now you are free of the stronghold.' The fading sunlight glinted on her hair and Banner looked away swiftly. He had already shown too much of his feelings.

'He'll decide for himself when he's old enough. I don't care what he becomes as long as I can still be proud of him. But he is going to need someone to model himself on for that. I get the impression that you don't think the major is the right kind of man to give him that guidance. Am I wrong?'

He shrugged deeply. 'None of my business. What happens after I get you back to Pine Tree is your decision, not mine.'

'My future was decided a long time ago, Matt,' she said quietly. 'I had no say in it.'

'You have a say in it now,' he said gently. 'You are not a kid any longer. This time you have to make your own decisions, and you have a lot of time to think about it.'

'My grandmother's word was law, Matt. She made a promise that I have to keep, no matter how I feel about it. Anyway, perhaps I'm not ready to make my own decisions yet. So much has happened that I don't think I am able to decide anything for myself. All my life it seems that decisions have been made for me and perhaps it is better that way.'

She looked at him closely. 'I've been thinking something else too, Matt. I have been thinking that there is something that you haven't yet told me. Is it something to do with that pack you keep in the corner over there?'

In answer to her question he moved to the far corner of the room, lifted the pack and placed it on the table before untying it. 'There are things in there you might need,' he said, stepping back to let her unwrap the bundle. 'I had to guess at the sizes.'

Tina unwrapped the bundle. A few dresses, a bonnet, a bundle of calico, needle, thread and scissors. 'You seem to have thought of everything, Banner,' she said coldly. 'Is there any reason why I can't wear the clothes I am wearing now back to Pine Tree?'

He shrugged. 'It's the way Buckman wants it. I just follow orders.'

'You have never followed orders in your life, Banner, other than those I have given you. Why does the major want me to wear these clothes?'

'He doesn't want anyone to know that you've been a Comanche prisoner. He told everyone that you were at an uncle's ranch in Sonora when the attack on Pine Tree took place.'

She looked angry, then confused. 'Why? For all he knew I could have been killed instead of kidnapped.'

'Cody didn't think so and, I guess, he trusted Cody's instincts.'

'It still doesn't answer my question, Banner. Why?'

'I guess he was thinking of you, giving you a chance at a new life without people talking about you behind your back.'

'You are a poor liar, Banner. I would be an embarrassment to him. Isn't that closer to the truth? The major wouldn't want people to think of him as a squawman. And that's what I am now, Mr Banner. Nothing more than a Comanche squaw. He's always been an ambitious man. Even as a young girl I realized that. Perhaps that was part of his attraction. I don't know. I suppose I should have expected it of him, but not of you. You disappoint me, Banner. You are the last person in the world I would expect to go along with something like this.'

He watched the moisture glisten in her eyes and ached to take her in his arms to try and ease her pain. 'I went along with him because I didn't know how you would feel about it. You know what people are like. Women are the meanest. A man can escape from the Comanche and he's a hero, but not a woman. People look at her differently. There's always going to be some female who is going to say she would rather slit her own throat than share a lodge with a Comanche buck. No decent woman would consider any other alternative. They are liars. Sometimes it takes more guts to go on living than take the easy way out. What you did took guts and don't let anyone tell you any different.'

He paused to pour coffee into two mugs. 'You wear what you want back to Pine Tree and I'll be proud to ride alongside you. Seems to me a man should always be proud to have you at his side, no matter what.'

His words disarmed her completely. Banner was a man of few words and even fewer compliments, but they were always honest. She was seeing a side of Matt Banner that no one else had ever been allowed to see. Her words were hesitant. 'And Bobby? Will he expect me to deny my own son?'

He put her coffee on the table before her. 'Maybe we are judging the major too quick. People change but they sometimes need a little help. Why don't we let Bobby handle Buckman? He seems to have a way with big, tough men.'

She knew what he meant. It had worked on Banner. Perhaps Bobby could also work his special charm on Major Buckman. They would have to wait and see. Buckman was in the past, a mere shadow, but Banner was here and now, a man of rare strength and character. Somehow she had severe doubts that any other man could live up to the standards Banner set for himself. All her misgivings about him and Bobby had vanished. Bobby was safer with Matt Banner than he would be with his own father. There was a special bond between them now and woe betide anyone who tried to sever that bond. Perhaps, if she wasn't already promised to the major things might have worked differently, but somehow she didn't think so.

Her parents, especially her father, would have approved of Matt Banner.

10

She heard the door close quietly behind Banner as she dressed quickly and moved into the main room. The early morning sun filtered softly through the windows; the first signs of spring were already in the air, and the thaw was setting in—to most people a new beginning, but not to her. She had come to love her life here. It had been a long time since since she had felt the warmth and security of four walls and the protection of a strong man willing to lay down his life to defend her.

There had been no love between her and Ghost Warrior. She was just a squaw to do his bidding and give him sons. If it wasn't for Bobby she doubted that he would even be out there looking for them now. Squaws were easy to come by as long as a man had enough ponies, but sons were to be treasured and prized above all else.

No, she decided suddenly, even if Bobby wasn't with them Ghost Warrior would still be out there looking for them. Banner had stolen his woman, and he would have to pay the price. No one, especially Banner, could ever be allowed to insult Ghost Warrior in such a way. Comanche Killer—she rarely thought of him that way any more—had issued a challenge to Ghost Warrior and he must respond.

Bobby was still fast asleep, would be for a long time yet. There was no sign of Banner at the stables, but his footprints led up the mountain. She found him up there, looking down into his valley, the place she was seeing for the first time. It was beautiful. She looked at his face. They had been together for a few months now and he no longer kept his thoughts private from her. She knew how he felt. She hadn't wanted the spring to arrive either. If it wasn't for Cody, Pine Tree could remain a part of her past. They could stay here. No one need ever know that Banner had rescued her from the stronghold.

No. That would never work. Banner had taken money to bring her back and he would never renege on that. She stood at his side, looking down into the valley. It would always be beautiful regardless of the season. She wished she could see the seasons in that valley for herself. She imagined that the Fall would be the most beautiful. She had no real wish to leave this place and knew he didn't either. If ... why should an old woman be allowed to dictate her granddaughter's future, even after her death? Perhaps things would change in time? She hoped so.

'How soon will the pass be open?' she asked, fearful of the answer.

He shrugged. 'A week. Ten days at the most. It's thawing fast.'

'You're a lucky man to be surrounded by so much beauty.'

'I guess I never really noticed it before,'

he said quietly. 'A man has to feel beauty inside him before he can really see it.'

'I envy you being able to come here whenever you want to.'

'I won't be coming back,' he said flatly, turning away and heading back to the cabin. She watched him, puzzled. How could a man walk away from such beauty so easily? Was it because of her? No, that was too much to hope for. There was no chance for them. She had a promise to keep, even if it was to a person long since dead.

Bobby was watching Banner closely. Something was bothering the big man, but he didn't know what. Tina was aware of it too. Again he was isolating himself from them, becoming his own man again. He spent as little time as possible in the cabin now, always finding things to do away from them. Yet she had the feeling that Banner was never far away. He would never leave them unprotected.

They would be leaving soon and the sense of security Tina had known here would vanish. She handed him a cup of coffee, her eyes searching his face for answers but finding nothing. The old Banner was back, cold and unyielding, his thoughts private and guarded. The man she had hoped never to see again was back, and she didn't like it.

He rolled a cigarette carefully, his voice barely audible when he spoke. 'The pass is open. We can move out in the morning.'

The fact that he was in such a hurry disturbed her. Was he that eager to get rid of them? She moved towards the bedroom. 'I'll get my things ready.' She paused in the doorway. 'I'm going to miss this place. It's the only home I've known for a long time. Nowhere else is ever going to feel the same.'

Banner got to his feet, his face and voice tight. 'It's a house, just like any other.'

'Like the one we passed on the way here?' she asked quietly. 'That burned-out shell? That was a house too, wasn't it? Someone must have lived in that house once. There were laughter and tears in that house. That's what makes it a home, Banner, not four walls and a roof. It must have hurt them to leave that house, too.'

'They didn't leave,' Banner said quietly. 'I buried them down there. My mother, father, kid brother and little sister. She was eight years old. I was up here when the Comanches hit. The night of the Comanche moon. When I got back it was too late. I was fifteen and I've been killing Comanches ever since. Does that answer the question you've been wanting to ask ever since I took you out of the stronghold?'

It answered a lot of questions about Matthew Banner. Ever since he had been a kid hate had been his only reason for living. Perhaps it still was, but she didn't think so. Here in this cabin, Banner had learned another way of life, with a little help from Bobby and herself. He had learned what it was like to be a part of a family again. Now, once more it was to taken from him. Would he be the same after this? She doubted it. Already she could envisage a foe that would give even Ghost Warrior nightmares. She went into the room, alone with her thoughts and tears. There would be no give in Banner now. He would get her back to Pine Tree, and stay around until he felt that there was no longer any danger of attack. He had already given her his word on that, but she would see little of him, and one day he would disappear without a word. It was Banner's way. He would revert back to his old way of life and many more Comanche would die ... until Banner himself was dead.

Banner moved cautiously, every sense alert, as they moved through the timber skirting the valley. Alone, he would have preferred to travel out in the open, relying on the speed of the big black to get him out of any trouble should he spot any Comanche. With the girl and the kid along it was safer to keep to cover.

Ghost Warrior was around somewhere. He knew it. He would have already checked Pine Tree to see if Banner had turned up there. Probably still had scouts there, making sure he would be informed if they arrived. Other braves would be watching Devlin. Ghost Warrior was no fool. Wherever Banner turned up, he would know soon afterwards. And there was little chance of slipping by them. Alone, it would have been easy, but with the girl and the kid along ...

As if reading his thoughts, she said, 'Where do you think he is?'

'Probably somewhere between us and Devlin. If not, he'll be waiting around Pine Tree.'

She looked alarmed. 'Don't worry,' he said softly. 'Ghost Warrior won't hit Pine Tree until after we get there. He wouldn't want us to get word of an attack on the ranch and disappear again. He wants us where he can find us and that's back at Pine Tree.'

'And when he does find us?' she asked quietly.

'Ghost Warrior is a proud man. Banner took his woman and his son. That makes it a personal fight. It will be between him and me. One of us will have to die. Maybe both.'

His quick eyes caught the smoke rising from a ridge and movement in the aspens opposite. 'It may be sooner than we think.'

11

Panic touched her voice. They had been so close. Just a few more days, that was all they needed. 'Do you think they have spotted us?'

He glanced back over his shoulder. 'That's answering smoke. Looks like someone on our back trail has spotted something, tracks, maybe. They know someone is around here, and they'll be coming at us from all sides now, closing in on us until they've got us boxed in. One thing is sure; they won't give in until they catch up with us.'

Her lovely eyes misted. For the past few days she had seen Pine Tree in her mind's eye, and heard Cody welcoming her home. But it wasn't to be. No more Pine Tree. It was all about to be taken from her.

And Banner would be dead. She would be back in the stronghold with no more hope of rescue.

Banner dead! She shuddered at the thought. Perhaps she could make a deal with Ghost Warrior. All he really wanted was his woman and son back, didn't he? If ...

She started to rein her horse away, holding tight to Bobby. If she could get to Ghost Warrior first.

'Don't even think about it,' Banner said harshly. 'You can't buy my life by going back to Ghost Warrior. He needs my scalp hanging from his war lance to prove he is the greatest warrior of them all. He can't take a chance on me riding back into the stronghold again.'

'Then what do we do?' she asked desperately.

He rolled a cigarette, scratching a match to flame on his pants leg. There was no way out. On his own he would have stood a chance, but with the girl and the boy along ... He wasn't about to leave them now. They had come too far.

He blew smoke towards the clear blue sky before answering. 'I guess I meet them head on.'

'Head on? You are crazy! One man against at least thirty. You won't stand a chance. They won't be shooting at Bobby and me. They will all be shooting at you. How can you hope to stand up to all those men alone?'

A sudden thought struck him. He didn't like the idea but there was no other way. 'I hope to cut those odds down, so don't be surprised or frightened by anything that happens.'

She followed, stunned, as he reined the big black to head down into the valley, in plain sight of any watching eyes. There wasn't even any cover when the trouble came, as come it would. Banner was crazy, driven by some strange impulse that she would never understand. All he wanted to do now was to die as he had lived, fighting

Comanches. She had been wrong; none of the hate had died in Banner, it just lay simmering beneath the surface.

They were in the open now, and already she could see the first signs of movement in the trees opposite. As the first of the Comanche appeared Banner reached across suddenly, plucking the boy from her arms and placing him on the saddle before him. His eyes narrowed as he watched over a dozen Comanche come into sight, moving carefully across the valley towards them, weapons at the ready.

Doubt clouded their painted faces. This was Comanche Killer, the invincible one, care must be taken. It was said that he could not be killed. Before this day ended it would be known if the legend of Banner was true.

Banner slid the big Colt into his hand, touching the muzzle against the boy's head. 'Come any closer and the boy dies,' he shouted, his voice carrying across the silent valley. He eased the hammer of his

Colt back to full-cock, the sound sending a chill through Tina's blood.

Banner's voice rose again, cold and deadly. 'Find Ghost Warrior. Tell him Banner is here with his son. If he does not come soon the boy will die at the hands of Comanche Killer.'

The unveiled threat frightened Tina. Was Banner really capable of murdering her son in cold blood? She couldn't be sure. Killing was second nature to Banner, had been for a very long time. After fifteen years human life meant little to Banner. But a boy? She thought he liked Bobby. It had seemed that Bobby had made Banner human again. But that was back in the cabin, and Banner had changed as soon as the spring had started to appear. Nothing showed in his face now. The face of a cold-blooded killer? She couldn't be sure any more.

The fact that he couldn't hope to take on all of Ghost Warrior's men bothered her. That was impossible, and he knew it. But Banner had a plan, and she knew exactly what that plan was. Banner had just one thing in mind: to kill Ghost Warrior before he himself died. She watched him closely, trying to read his mind. Did he really intend killing Bobby or offering the boy's life in exchange for his father's? Yes. Banner would think that way. The fact that he would die soon afterwards wouldn't mean much to Comanche Killer. He would have achieved his goal. More movement distracted her and she recognized the imposing figure of Ghost Warrior.

Tall for a Comanche, Ghost Warrior pulled the handsome paint horse to a halt, his eyes set upon the tall man aboard the black in the distance. Banner had returned. Somehow he had always known it would be so. He had seen it in his dreams. Banner and he would fight, and one of them would die. It was meant to be. But could one fight an immortal and hope to live?

With his own eyes, Ghost Warrior had seen Banner leap into the river of death, but Banner was here, and had once more entered the stronghold to steal his wife and son. How could this be? No other had survived the river of death, but Comanche Killer had returned from the dark land beyond life. Somehow he had always known it would be so. It was spoken in his dreams. Today one of them would die. The man who lived would be the greatest warrior of them all.

He glanced over his shoulder and read the fear in the faces of his men. Banner was an immortal. How could Ghost Warrior fight him and hope to survive? Immortals could not be killed. He fought his own fear as he looked again at Banner. It was already written and there was nothing he could do about it.

Would Banner kill his son? He did not know. Banner hated all the Comanche, many had died at his hands, yet there was respect in Ghost Warrior for his old enemy. Banner was neither a fool or a coward. Today one of them would die, but that man would die with honour.

Signalling his men to stay behind, Ghost Warrior advanced slowly down into the valley.

12

Ghost Warrior stopped about twenty feet from Banner. The boy and his woman looked well. For a second his hard features softened as he looked at the boy. The flint was back in his eyes when they came to rest on Banner.

'Does Banner now threaten children?' he asked flatly.

'It brought you here,' Banner answered softly. 'That is all that matters.'

Ghost Warrior nodded. 'Banner wishes Ghost Warrior to offer his own life in exchange for his son's? It shall be so.'

'Banner wishes only to talk. The woman belongs with her own people. It is the reason I came back to the stronghold. And the boy belongs with his mother. If I do not take her back with me the pony soldiers will come instead.'

'Banner is the only white who knows the way to the stronghold. With him dead, there will be no one to lead the pony soldiers to the stronghold. Banner was foolish to come after the woman.'

'Ghost Warrior is the fool. He thinks only of himself and not of his people. If Banner does not take the girl back, the pony soldiers will come. They will have no need to find their way into the stronghold. They have only to surround it. It will then become a trap for Ghost Warrior. They will have many guns and much food. They will wait there until they hear the cries of women and children with empty bellies. Would Ghost Warrior let his people starve to death rather than surrender? I think not.'

'Perhaps it will be as Banner says but Comanche Killer will not live to see that day. Banner will die here at the hands of Ghost Warrior.' He touched his knife for emphasis. 'The death of Banner will prove to be the strongest medicine of all. The story will be told and many more warriors will join with me. The Comanche will be the most powerful of all the tribes. Banner must die to prove that Ghost Warrior is truly the invincible one.'

Banner shook his head reluctantly. He hadn't wanted it to come to this but had always known it was inevitable. Ghost Warrior and he had been born to tangle, and there was no way to avoid it.

'And if Banner should win?' Banner asked quietly. 'Will Ghost Warrior's braves let him ride from this place with the woman and boy?'

'Ghost Warrior's word is law. Should Banner defeat me he will be free to ride from this place. No Comanche hand will be raised against him.'

'And the woman and the boy?' Banner persisted.

'If it is what the woman and the boy want, it shall be so.'

'It is what we wish,' Tina said softly.

He nodded, satisfied. 'It is good. A woman and boy will not want with Banner to care for them.' He raised his voice suddenly. 'Hear the words of Ghost Warrior. In this place, at this time, I will fight with Banner. Should Banner win he will be free to leave with my woman and my son. No Comanche hand will be raised against him. This is the word of Ghost Warrior. His word must not be broken.'

He dismounted, letting his fine-looking paint horse roam free as he stripped to the waist. His body was even more powerful than Banner remembered, the muscles standing out like thick ropes against his chest and arms. Only the bowed legs spoiled the illusion. The Comanche were the centaurs among Indians, half-man, half horse. For an instant Banner wondered what the Comanche were like before they discovered horses? Tall and proud like the Cheyenne? Somehow he doubted it.

Banner dismounted, taking the boy with him. His face sombre, he handed Bobby up to Tina. 'Get him away from here, Tina. I don't want him to see this.'

Her hand touched his face gently. 'There is no other way, is there, Matt?'

He shook his head. 'I didn't want this, Tina. Believe me.'

'I know, Matt. We'll wait in the timber for you.'

She reined her horse away quickly. Strangely, there was no fear in her for Matt Banner, just regret that he was being forced into a fight that he didn't want. For the first time in his life, Banner had no wish to kill a Comanche.

He had been in knife fights before. She knew that from the scars on his body when she had treated him back in the cabin. She glanced back to see him slip that wicked-looking Bowie knife into his hand. Like the black Colt it was a part of the man. The fact that Bobby's father would probably die at Banner's hands disturbed her. Just as it would bother Matt Banner.

Ghost Warrior faced his greatest foe

impassively. Comanche Killer's name was legendary among his people. Banner had returned from Hell, to add to the legend. Banner must die here, before his people, to destroy the myth forever. Ghost Warrior would kill him and become the greatest of all the Comanche or any other tribe. Banner must die: there could be no other outcome to the duel.

He watched Banner move forward, light on his feet, the big blade held easy and relaxed in his hand. There was an intensity to Banner that he had never noticed. Before, Banner had been merely a prisoner in the stronghold, someone to amuse the squaws. The sight of Banner being whipped and fighting the dogs for scraps had amused the braves, too. Yet, Banner had never been defeated, Ghost Warrior realized that now. Even in death, his name would live for ever among the Comanche. Longer even than Ghost Warrior's, unless he defeated Comanche Killer here today.

'Banner would not have killed my son,'

he said suddenly. 'Banner is weak now, because he no longer hates.'

'I learned something, Ghost Warrior: love is stronger than hate. It gives a man a reason to live. Hate only destroys a man. That is something we must all learn.'

'My hate for the white man makes me strong, Banner. I will not rest until they are all dead or driven from the land of the Comanche. Banner is the only white man worthy of respect, but he must die also.'

'Not today, Ghost Warrior. Today is not Banner's day to die. Banner has learned to live again.'

He moved swiftly aside, light and easy on his feet, as Ghost Warrior's blade flashed towards him. The brave was faster than he imagined, but he was ready. Banner had never been one to underestimate an opponent, and Ghost Warrior had a big reputation among knife fighters. Still, Banner had one advantage: Ghost Warrior being a Comanche had spent most of his life aboard a horse. Banner had spent a lot of time walking and climbing, giving his legs an agility that Ghost Warrior could never hope to match. As a boy, Banner had done a lot of exploring among the forests and in the mountains. He had learned to walk soft not to disturb the animals and watch the ground as he walked. It was a lesson well learned. Even now, he knew every rock and patch of uneven ground where they fought.

Ghost Warrior advanced quickly, locking knife blades with Banner. Locked together, they tested each other's strength. Banner was much stronger than the Comanche imagined, different from the man he had known back in the stronghold. Surprised, he found himself being forced backwards. That would not look good to his people. He broke away, his knife flashing to disembowel Banner, but the white man had anticipated it, moving swiftly aside. Still, first blood to Ghost Warrior as the blade slashed across Banner's ribs. Not serious, but it gave his foe fresh heart.

He came forward, his blade flashing like lightning, a smile on his face. A few more cuts like that would weaken Banner, and he would be easy prey.

His smile broadened as he drove Banner back. His blade had taught Banner respect for the greatest warrior of them all. He was confident now. Soon Comanche Killer's scalp would be hanging from his war lance for all to see. Many would come to the stronghold to see it. Already he could sense victory. Banner was still backing up with something akin to fear. But it was a short-lived victory. Banner was advancing again, confident, the blade deadly and eager in his hand, He feinted towards Ghost Warrior's ribs. The Comanche moved quickly aside, his knife flashing towards Banner, but the big man was no longer there. Perhaps Banner was a ghost, after all? No, ghosts did not bleed, and he had Banner's blood on his blade. Banner feinted again at Ghost Warrior's right side. The Comanche moved to counter the move but Banner had fooled him. With an easy practised move, Banner had switched the Bowie knife to his left hand.

There was no pain and he heard rather than felt Banner's blade sink deeply into his stomach. As if in a dream, he watched Banner withdraw the heavy blade, red with the life blood from his body. He felt the strength drain from his body and he sank to his knees. Banner was beside him but, strangely, there was no joy of victory on Comanche Killer's face. Why? Banner should be happy. He had defeated his greatest enemy, proved himself the finest warrior of them all.

'Banner is a great warrior,' he said weakly. 'He will teach my son well. My son will learn to walk the warrior's path, and Banner will teach him the way of the Comanche. Banner knows the Comanche ways better than any white man.'

'There will be no warrior's path for your son, Ghost Warrior. Whichever way he turns he will be fighting against his own people. This must not be.'

'Comanche blood is strong, Banner. My son was born to fight. When the time is right, he will take my place.'

'Not against white men, Ghost Warrior. They cannot be defeated. There are too many. Each day more arrive. They are as many as the leaves on the trees in the summer. In the Fall, the leaves die, but each spring they start to appear again. It is the same with the white man.'

Pain flashed across Ghost Warrior's face. 'Perhaps Banner is right, but would Banner want the Comanche to live like cowards and beg food from the white man?'

'No, Ghost Warrior. I want the Comanche to learn the ways of the white man, and for the white man to learn the ways of the Comanche. Only when we understand each other can we live side by side.'

Ghost Warrior looked puzzled. This was not the Banner he had once known. 'Hate has died in Banner. This I saw and thought it made Banner weak, but I was wrong. Banner is now stronger than ever. My son will have a good father. He will teach my son the ways of the Comanche, and my son will learn respect for his people. I would want no other to take my place. Banner will raise my son and care for him as his own. This I see.'

Banner searched for the right words to help Ghost Warrior understand his real purpose for being here. 'I had a job to do. I cannot make any promises. Once I get the woman back to her people ...'

Ghost Warrior's breath was shallow now as he struggled to speak. 'My son is now your son. No one ...'

His voice trailed off and he died. Slowly Banner got to his feet, not liking himself. It was almost as if Ghost Warrior had extracted an unspoken promise from him, a promise that he couldn't keep. The boy was someone else's problem, not his. Another man's responsibility, even though he didn't like entrusting that responsibility to Buckman. He didn't think that Buckman would take too kindly to having a half-breed Comanche for a son.

The sound of hoofbeats disturbed him and he looked up to see himself surrounded by twenty warriors. He resisted glancing at his gun belt still hanging from the black's saddle horn. He wouldn't make it. Even if he could, the odds were against him. The best he could hope for was to take a few more Comanche with him as he died. Either way, the outcome would be the same: he would be dead and Tina and the boy on their way back to the stronghold. He straightened, resigned to his fate. There had been enough killing for one day.

'Ghost Warrior is dead,' he said quietly.

Two Ponies nodded. 'It shall be told.'

'Let it be known that Comanche Killer is also dead.'

Two Ponies looked pleased. One of the greatest threats to the Comanche had been removed. 'It shall be told.' He looked down sadly at the body of Ghost Warrior. 'Perhaps the day of the warrior is over. Banner spoke of the pony soldiers, of the day when they would come to the stronghold. There was truth in his words. The Comanche must learn to live with the white man or face defeat. But there is no honour in surrender.'

'I spoke not of surrender, but of peace among us. The pony soldiers will honour a treaty of peace with the Comanche. There will be beef and clothing so that the women and young ones will not go hungry or cold. A wise chief will lead his people to the path of peace.'

Two Ponies eyes searched Banner's face and found truth. Banner spoke well and there was wisdom in his words. 'Banner would speak with the chief of the pony soldiers and tell him that the Comanche have a new leader who wishes to speak with him of peace.'

'This I will do. I will tell them that

Two Ponies is a wise chief who speaks with honest words.'

He moved towards his horse, swinging easily into the saddle, leaving his gun belt hooked over the saddle horn. To buckle on the belt now would show distrust in the Comanche word, and that would never do. He rode away without looking back. Even though Ghost Warrior was dead, his word was still law, and he had promised Banner safe passage from this place. Two Ponies would kill any man who tried to break the word of Ghost Warrior. Only when he reached the timber, did Banner fasten on his gun belt. He felt naked without it.

Tina waited anxiously. Banner was a man who inspired confidence, but accidents happened, and he was only one man against twenty. As yet, she hadn't heard any gunshots, and that was a good sign. Banner would never go down without a fight.

It seemed that her heart started beating

again as she recognized the big black weaving its way towards them through the trees. Her lovely eyes questioned him as he stopped before them.

'It's over,' he said quietly. 'Two Ponies is now chief. He wants to talk peace with the commander of the fort. Ghost Warrior ...' He let the words trail off.

She had already read the truth in his face. The death of Ghost Warrior saddened him as it saddened her. He had been her husband and the father of her son. The fact that there had been no love between them, or even affection, softened the blow for her, but she hated what it was doing to Banner. A few months ago Banner would have enjoyed the sight of Ghost Warrior lying dead at his feet, but not now. He had changed. He no longer enjoyed killing Comanches.

Her eyes came to rest on his blood-soaked shirt, and gasped. 'You've been hurt. Let me take a look.'

He shook his head. 'Not yet. There's an

old adobe a few miles from here. We'll rest up there for a day or two. I want to make sure that all the Comanches know that we've been granted safe passage before we head back to Pine Tree.'

He glanced back at the far side of the valley. Already the smoke signals were rising in the distance, telling of Ghost Warrior's death and that Banner was not to be harmed. But it would take at least a day before he would feel safe again. His quick ears caught the sudden patter of rain on the leaves, and he glanced upwards. Looked like it would be heavy. He hoped that old adobe still had at least part of its roof.

His wish had been granted, he thought wryly as they came within sight of the house. Part of the roof sagged in one corner, but still looked waterproof, as long as they stayed out of that corner. He got a fire going before letting Tina attend to his wound. Thankfully it wasn't deep, and she had brought bandages from the cabin. Somehow she'd had the feeling that Banner would always be in need of medical help.

He shrugged back into a fresh shirt, his face thoughtful. She watched him carefully. Banner had been that way ever since leaving the cabin, aloof and distant. Was it because he knew that he would soon be forced to part company with Bobby and her? She could hardly hope for that. Banner was a loner when she had first met him, never needing or wanting anyone. It would be easy for him to revert back to type. She would miss him far more than he would ever miss her. She would never hear the words from him that she wanted to hear.

With the threat of a Comanche raid against Pine Tree hanging over them, she had had at least the promise of him staying around the ranch for a while. Now that threat no longer existed. He would only stay around long enough to pick up the rest of his money before riding out of her life forever. Money! That was all she and Bobby meant to him, all they would ever mean to him.

'How will you spend the money, Banner?' she asked suddenly.

He looked puzzled, wondering what she meant.

'The money you'll get for taking us back to Pine Tree. That is all you really care about, isn't it? I thought you had changed, thought you had learned to care about something other than killing Comanches. I was wrong. Money is now everything to you, isn't it?'

'It has its uses,' Banner said quietly, moving towards the rain-swept window. It wasn't in him to explain his motives. Women never understood the workings of a man's mind anyway. They were a separate species. Heavy clouds drifted across the night sky as he looked out, the rain getting heavier as if intent upon washing away the last of the winter snow.

'We should never have left the cabin,' she said wistfully. 'I felt that Bobby and I had someone up there who really cared about us. How many mistakes can one woman make?'

'You have a promise to keep, and so have I,' he said softly. 'Neither of us can go beyond that.'

'Someone else made that promise for me, Matt. I had no say in it.'

'But you'll abide by it, the same way that I'll stick to my word. We don't have any choice.'

He was right, even though she hated to admit it. Running away from any problem never solved it. Sooner or later that problem would arise again. Anyway she wasn't even sure that Banner cared enough about Bobby and her to make any real commitment to them. And that was one question she could never ask him. She didn't know what really went on in his mind and probably never would.

There was no longer any way to reach

Matt Banner, she realized sadly. He would fulfil his promise to Major Buckman, and disappear from her life as suddenly as he had appeared in it.

13

The sight she had yearned to see for so long, now filled her with dread. Pine Tree was no longer her home. Home was Banner's cabin back there in the mountains. Memories of the Comanche attack on Pine Tree still lived with her, still brought tears to her eyes. Always would. She would no longer feel safe there, unless ... no, it was a feeble hope. Banner would only stay around long enough to collect his money from the major before riding out again.

Even now with the Comanche threat at an end she would no longer feel safe anywhere without Banner close by. Her first sight of that spectre-like figure appearing out of nowhere still haunted her, but even then she had felt his strength. Without him, without that strength ... the thought made her shudder. The cruel fact was that Banner had become a part of her life, but he would never allow her to become part of his. That hurt more deeply than she cared to admit.

Was love always like this, she wondered, needing someone so badly that nothing else mattered, even her own pride? Love? Was it possible? Was she in love with Banner? No. It couldn't be. Must not be. Loving Banner meant only pain. Love was sharing; thoughts, feelings, emotions and she wasn't sure that Banner had any real emotions. He was a man alone, a man who needed to live his own life in his own way. In Banner's book, needing someone was a weakness. There was no room for Bobby and her in his life.

She watched him now, stern-faced and private as she had first known him. The real Matt Banner. He was looking straight ahead. How far before they reached the ranch? Another eight, ten miles? She couldn't remember. For some strange reason she felt frightened. Banner had distanced himself from them already, and it was if they had never existed for him. Still, he had the scars from the bullet wound and his fight to remind him. All she had was a memory, but that would never fade. She was sure of that now. She touched Bobby's face gently. The boy, too, was puzzled by Banner's conduct, his change of attitude towards them. Perhaps when he was older she would be able to find the right words to explain Banner's behaviour? She hoped so. Bobby needed to be told the truth about Banner. She owed him at least that much.

'We're on Pine Tree land,' he told her needlessly, a certain regret in his voice. Or was that just her imagination?

She knew this land. Every inch of it had been covered by Cody and her. This ranch had been a part of her every dream over the past nine years. Now those dreams had become reality. Somehow the dreams were better.

Even the thought of seeing Cody again disturbed her. Would she still recognize him? She thought so. Cody had the kind of face that would never change much. She reined in suddenly. 'How long will you be staying?'

'I'll drop you off at Pine Tree, and pick up the rest of my money from Buckman. I'll call back at Pine Tree before crossing the Rio.'

'Are you that anxious to get your money, Matt? You said you would stay around Pine Tree for a while, for as long as we needed you. I thought you always kept your word, Matt?'

'You had the threat of a Comanche attack hanging over you then. That threat no longer exists. I'm not needed any more.'

'We still need you, Matt,' she said quietly. 'Perhaps more than ever I need you, Matt. I'm scared of facing people again. From here on I'll be living a lie, but lies have a way of sneaking up on people, lurking around every corner, waiting to catch up on us. How long do you think it will be before they find out the truth about me?'

He shrugged. 'I don't know, Tina, but I am sure of one thing: you'll face up to it with the same kind of courage you had when you were a captive of the Comanche. They couldn't break you then, and they won't break you now.'

'I was alone then, Matt, no one else to turn to. I didn't have your strength to feed off. You made the difference. Relying on someone else saps your own strength. That is something that you know better than anyone else. That's why you chose the way of life you have. I'm not like you, Matt. I need someone else to lean on. I'm afraid of living a lie. Every day I will be afraid that someone will expose me.'

'Then don't live a lie, Tina. If you want to put on that Comanche dress again and ride in to Pine Tree, I'll ride right alongside you, and I'll be proud to do it.'

'I know, Matt,' she said gently. 'But I can't just think of myself, can I? I have to think of Bobby, the kind of life he'd have as the son of a Comanche among white children. The hates of the fathers will be passed on to the sons. Isn't that the way things will happen, Matt?'

He nodded. 'It's the way of things, Tina. If I had ever had a son I guess I would have brought him up to hate Comanches, too.'

His frankness told her that hate for all things Comanche had died within him. He rolled a cigarette, scratching a match to flame on his pants leg. 'Cody will help you, Tina. He's a good man. He cares a lot about you, and he'll grow to love Bobby. It won't take him long.'

'Cody isn't you, Matt,' she said softly. 'He can't teach Bobby the things you can. We need more time with you.' She paused.

'There's a line cabin a few miles from here. It was never used this time of year. We could spend the night there together, just the three of us. We can ride to the ranch in the morning. Just one more day out of your life, Matt. Is that too much to ask?'

'The problem won't go away overnight, Tina. But I guess one more day won't make that much difference to either of us. I doubt if Buckman is that eager to part with his money anyway.'

'Everything comes down to money with you, doesn't it, Matt? Or perhaps you just enjoy the thought of taking it off Major Buckman?'

'My promise ends when I get you back to the ranch, Tina. Your promise begins then. There's nothing I can do about that.'

'We could go back to the cabin, Matt. We were happy there.'

'Spend the rest of your life without seeing people, Tina? You couldn't live like that. And I wouldn't want you to.

You'll spend the rest of your life knowing that you broke your grandmother's word, and feeling guilty about it. Sooner or later you would start taking it out on the kid and me. I could live with it, maybe, but it wouldn't be fair on the boy. You have to face up to the situation and make the decision on your own.'

'I don't know if I'm capable of making a decision on my own any more, Matt. I need help, and I'm not too proud to ask you for it.'

'You are asking the wrong man, Tina. I can't make decisions for anyone else. I've been on my own for too long. The cabin looks good to you now, but it won't always be that way. You'll be a prisoner up there the same as you were in the stronghold, and you'll blame me for keeping you there. You will grow to hate me, and there's no getting around that. My way is best. I take you back to Pine Tree, and then ride away. You belong among people. You've lost so much of your youth that you have a lot of catching up to do. That's something you can't do in the mountains.'

He blew smoke at the sky. 'I'll take you back to Pine Tree, pick up my money from Buckman and then ride away. But if you ever really need me, Cody will know where to find me.'

She hid her tearstained face from him. 'At least, you will get something out of this, Matt. Ten thousand dollars. Wasn't that the price for bringing me back? I'll have a husband who doesn't love me. Oh, I know the major's reason for wanting me back, Matt. He wants to get his hands on Pine Tree. That's all he really cares about, but I thought you were different, did things for principle not money. At least, I know where I stand with Buckman.'

She shook her head sadly. 'You're heading back into that black hole again, Matt, but this time there is no way out for you. You are the loser, not me. I'll have a son who loves me and I'll have Cody. Who will you have, Banner? No one. I like to think that we taught you to care, but I'm not sure now. Even your own life has no real meaning for you now.' She urged her horse forward. 'I think I'd like to go back to Pine Tree now. You were right about one thing: there is no sense in trying to hide from others ... or ourselves.'

14

Something akin to shock registered on Jack Stagg's face as they watched Banner dismount and come into the ranch-house. He hadn't expected to see him again. In fact he would have bet against it. But Banner was back and he didn't like it. How much did he know? Unconsciously, his hand moved closer to his gunbutt. If trouble came, he wanted to be ready. He breathed a sigh of relief as Banner ignored him and faced Buckman. 'I've come for the rest of my money, Buckman. The girl is back at Pine Tree with Cody.'

'It took you a long time, Banner.'

'I ran into a little trouble. Sometimes things don't go according to plan, do they, Stagg?'

The sudden question startled Stagg. 'Am

I supposed to understand that, Banner?'

'I think you do,' Banner said, turning back to Buckman. 'About that money ...?'

'I haven't seen the girl yet, Banner. Maybe you are lying or maybe you got the wrong girl. Either way, I'd like to see for myself.'

'You should never accuse a man of lying, Buckman. That's gun talk, and I doubt if you are good enough to back it up. That's the reason you hired the likes of Jack Stagg. 'Course if you find out that I'm lying, you can always send Stagg after me. He'd like that. So would I.'

He watched Buckman move quickly towards the safe. He pushed the money into his shirt with his left hand, his eyes never leaving Jack Stagg.

'That trouble you had, Banner ... what was it?'

'Two men decided they wanted to take over my job. They knew who I was and what I was doing in the Lost River country. Probably knew how much I was carrying, too. Only three men knew about me and my reason for being in the Lost River country. Cody, I trust, so that just leaves you and Stagg. I'm putting my money on Stagg.'

Buckman glanced angrily at Stagg. 'Me, too, Banner. You want to explain yourself, Stagg?'

'I didn't trust him to bring the girl back alone. Thought he might need some back-up. How could I know that the two men I hired would take things into their own hands? All I told them to do was cover Banner's back, help out if he needed it.'

'Very commendable, Jack, if I choose to believe it. You work for me, Stagg, you don't think for me. I assume that the two men you sent after Banner are dead. You could be next. I'm surprised that Banner hasn't killed you already.'

'He isn't good enough,' Stagg said softly, his cruel eyes boring into Banner.

'We'll find out soon enough,' Banner said quietly. 'Like I said, Buckman, the girl's back at Pine Tree, if you want to ride over that way later. She's got her son with her.'

His last sentence cut the air like a knife. Faintly amused, he watched Buckman's reaction. His words had hit the big man hard.

'Her son? She's got a kid? You brought a half-breed Comanche kid back here? You knew my plan, Banner. Tina was supposed to have been in Mexico for the past nine years and now she suddenly appears with a half-breed son? How am I supposed to explain that? You should have left the boy behind or smashed his head in with a rock.'

'His mother didn't see it that way, and I never argue with a woman, there's no way of winning. Besides, killing the boy would have made his father very angry.'

'Who the hell cares what one lousy Comanche thinks? One Comanche buck won't make any difference.'

'It would; his name was Ghost Warrior.

185

Tina was married to him, the boy is his son.'

Buckman swore loudly. 'Damn. That changes everything. I thought things had been too quiet around here lately. No Comanche raids reported for months either side of the border. That's the reason. He's had every man out looking for you. What happens next, Banner? How soon can we expect him to attack Pine Tree again? It's a sure thing that he knows the girl is back home. How soon before he hits?'

'Ghost Warrior is dead. I killed him. Two Ponies is now chief of the Comanche. He's chosen the path of peace.'

Relief flooded through Buckman. Without the Comanche threat hanging over them, life was going to get a lot easier. He could concentrate on merging his ranch and Pine Tree. The boy was a problem, but the answer to that was already forming in his mind. Jack Stagg would start earning his keep again, if Banner didn't kill him before he left.

'That was your real reason for going back to the Lost River, to kill Ghost Warrior, wasn't it, Banner?'

'I thought so, Buckman. But when it came right down to it, I didn't want to do it. I learned things, a lot of things that I didn't know before. People change, but only if they are big enough to take a long hard look at themselves.'

He turned abruptly, heading towards the door. 'By the way, Buckman, the girl is fine, in case you were wondering. She deserves better than you, but that's something that she will have to face up to for herself.' He paused with his hand on the latch. 'Today is your lucky day, Stagg. Next time I see you I'll kill you.'

Tina rushed quickly into the yard as she heard the sound of hoofbeats moving quickly away from Pine Tree. Dark clouds drifted across the evening sky but there was no mistaking that tall dark figure aboard the big black horse. Banner. He was leaving ... heading back across the Rio to disappear from her life again for ever. He was leaving without even saying goodbye to Bobby and her. But that was Banner's way, and he would never change.

She sensed rather than saw Cody's presence at her side. 'Where does he live, Cody? Is there any way of reaching him?'

'Physically or mentally?' he asked quietly. 'I think you and Bobby reached him, if that's what you mean. He's a hard man to understand. I guess that's a privilege that few people are allowed. You and Bobby are two of the lucky ones. You are probably the only two people in the world that he really cares about.'

'You're wrong, Cody. All Banner cares about is money. It's the only reason he came after me in the stronghold.'

'Could there be another reason, Tina? He didn't know you. And there are still a lot of white women captives among the Comanche, Kiowa and Apache. Why should you be so special to him? He hadn't even heard of you until I crossed the border and told him about you. It took a lot of courage for him to go back into the Lost River stronghold. He said the words that I thought I would never hear Banner say. He told me he was scared to go back there. He was afraid to face Ghost Warrior again, but he did it for you and Bobby. He wanted you to have a fresh start in life.'

'He did it for the money, Cody. He admitted as much to me.'

'He had a use for the money, Tina. You know where that money is now? It's in the bank, helping to pay off the bank loan on this place. The other five thousand he gave me tonight will clear that loan and make Pine Tree solvent again. That's how much money means to Banner. He hasn't made one cent out of bringing you and Bobby back. You don't owe anyone anything ... except him.'

15

Buckman swore bitterly. Damn Banner
anyway. The kid was going to be a
problem, and it was all Banner's fault.
Banner had known his plans, known his
ambition. Once the boy opened his mouth
about living in the stronghold and being the
son of Ghost Warrior, it was all over. The
damn fool should have left the kid in the
stronghold and ignored the girl's protests.
Banner never gave a damn what anyone
thought about him anyway.

Damn Jack Stagg, too, for not hiring
better men. If his hired guns had done
their job properly, Banner would be dead
back there in the Lost River country. The
kid, too. The kind of men Stagg would
hire wouldn't drag a kid along with them.
That would have solved a lot of problems.

Somewhere along the line they would have met up with Stagg and handed the girl over to him. Soon after Stagg would have killed them. The less people who knew where the girl had come from the better. Anyway, Stagg wouldn't have liked parting with his own money to pay a couple of cheap gunmen.

It would have been a good plan, had it worked, Buckman thought. Stagg had more brains than he had ever given him credit for. There was no doubt that Stagg had his sights set on the advance money he had paid Banner for going after the girl, but it was hardly likely that Banner had that money with him when he entered the stronghold. He smiled wryly. Stagg hadn't thought that far ahead.

Buckman lit a cigar before turning his attention to Jack Stagg. He had been quiet too long, and that bothered the half-breed. Maybe he was thinking about Stagg's attempted double-cross by hiring the two men to take Banner out? Hell, he had already explained that. Sure it was all a pack of lies, but they sounded good, and in the long run he was saving Buckman five thousand bucks. That should be worth something.

'I have a problem, Stagg,' Buckman said.

'If it's about me sending those two men after Banner ...'

'No, Stagg. It's the boy. He could ruin everything I've planned for. I don't like the idea of anyone or anything getting in my way.'

'No one need know that he's half-Comanche, Major. With his haircut, he looks just like any Mexican kid.'

'And when he starts talking about living in the stronghold, Stagg, speaking Comanche or telling other kids when he meets up with them that his father was the great Ghost Warrior? Other kids will laugh at him for a while, but maybe their parents won't. I can't take that chance, Stagg.' He poured himself a drink, before turning back to Stagg. 'He's a five-year-old kid, Stagg. Kids have accidents. They go places they shouldn't, like along a river bank. They stumble, fall, split their heads open on a rock or maybe fall into the river and get drowned. No one can keep their eyes on a kid all the time. They got a habit of sneaking away when no one is looking. Like I said, Stagg, accidents happen.'

He downed his brandy in one swallow and moved towards the safe. There was no need for further words.

Billy Todd pulled his horse to a stop, his face tight. He wasn't looking forward to breaking the bad news, but this was a job he couldn't handle on his own. He was going to need all the help he could get, and Cody would have his scalp if he didn't do it now. The sound of happy music coming from the town hall made it worse. One moment happiness, next moment, nothing, just an empty void inside.

His quick eyes sought out and found

Cody near the punch bowl, watching Tina dance with the major, a frown on Cody's tired face. To most people they made a handsome couple but not to Cody. To let her marry Buckman was tantamount to sending her back to the stronghold. He swore silently. Somehow he had to make her see sense, but Tina wasn't a kid any more. She had to make her own decisions. Maybe if Banner was still around? But Banner wasn't here. He was back in his own private stronghold south of the border, and knowing the big man was probably getting ready to move on again.

Where to? Someplace deeper into Mexico, further away from people, he guessed. The Mexicanos didn't ask too many questions, and gave Banner the privacy he sought. There was no reason for Banner to come back here, and the big man had to have a reason for doing anything, even if it made sense only to himself. Still he felt it would make a difference if Banner were here.

He felt the hand touch his shoulder

and turned to face Billy Todd. The youth looked worried. Damn! What now? Trouble at the ranch? Comanches? No. Banner had said that the Comanche threat had ended and he had never found any reason to doubt his word.

'It won't go away, boy. Get it said,' he snapped.

'The boy's missing, Cody. He was playing in a downstairs room when Maria went to cook his supper. When she came back, the window was open and the boy was gone. I tried tracking him, but nothing. It's raining pretty hard out there. If he left any tracks, I couldn't find them.'

Cody swore bitterly and looked around for Tina. She was talking to a couple of other women, but her thoughts were elsewhere. Back in that mountain cabin with Banner, he wondered?

He moved towards her quickly, his face betraying him. There was trouble, she could read it in his face. Bobby! It could only be Bobby.

'Bobby's missing, Tina. He must have slipped out the house through a window when no one was looking.' He grabbed her shoulders as her lovely face blanched. 'I'll round up every available man and go looking for him. We'll find him, Tina. I promise you.'

Buckman moved quickly to her side. 'My men will help, too. Those that are still sober enough to stay in a saddle.'

He moved away towards Jack Stagg. As yet, Stagg's partner in the night's work hadn't turned up. But that didn't matter. Brody would turn up when he was ready. It looked like the two men had handled the job well. There was little chance of anyone finding any tracks in the night, and with this weather ... even if Stagg and Brody had left any. A good job. The boy had been a threat and that threat had been removed. There was nothing between him and what he wanted now. Nothing.

Cody glanced at Tina. The long night had

taken its toll. She had insisted upon riding with them all through that long night. With the dawn, the rain had died out. He passed her a cup of coffee, his face tight. Buckman hovered near the fireplace. It had been a long night for him, too, and the man wasn't used to being out in the weather. The plain truth was the major didn't give a damn if the boy was found or not, but he had to put on a show. That's all he ever was and ever would be, Cody thought angrily, a damned showman.

'One of the boys found a feather out by the stables, Tina. He thinks it might be Comanche. Thinks maybe they came back here to pick up the boy and take him back to the stronghold.'

'No, Cody. Banner had Ghost Warrior's and Two Ponies' word that the boy would be safe.'

'Ghost Warrior is dead, Tina,' he reminded her gently. 'His word doesn't mean much any more.'

'Like my grandmother's?' she asked

quietly, glancing at Buckman, but the man was too busy with his own thoughts to hear her. The feather had been a clever touch on Stagg's part. The search had just about come to an end, following the finding of the feather. The boy's body would only be found by accident—if it ever was. He hadn't bothered to ask Stagg what he had done with the boy. Never would. It didn't matter.

'I can't believe that Two Ponies would break his word or Ghost Warrior's to Banner,' she said. 'The Comanche know what breaking their word to Banner would mean. They couldn't take a chance on that.'

Cody shrugged. 'They might, if they thought it would bring Comanche Killer back to the stronghold. Next time they would be waiting for him, if he was crazy enough to go back there.'

'He would go back if he was sure that the Comanches had Bobby, Cody,' she said softly. Even the mention of Banner's name inspired a great confidence in her. He would come back now. He had to.

'Send for him, Cody. Tell him what's happened. If anyone can find Bobby it's Banner.'

Buckman felt himself pale and turned away until he regained his colour. Banner was trouble. If he came back he wouldn't rest until he had found out what had happened to the boy. Banner was tough, dangerous and nobody's fool. He felt better when he heard Cody speak.

'He may not still be there, Tina. Banner doesn't like to stay in one place for too long, and I had the feeling that he was getting ready to move on again when he left here. It's a long shot, Tina.'

'Do we have any other choice?' she asked him quietly.

16

Banner moved quickly towards the rifle standing near the mine entrance. Someone was coming. The sudden raising of the black's head had warned him. He moved to the top of the narrow path—it could hardly be called a trail. Very few men knew the way to Banner's silver mine. He had discovered it a long time ago. He was hardly likely to get rich from it, but it gave him something to do, and swinging a pick put strength in his shoulders and arms. Over the years he had built up a tidy hoard of silver, but the mine had just about petered out now. Soon be time to move on. A change of scenery and maybe a change of name.

The cabin held a lot of good memories for him, but that was the reason he couldn't go back there.

He relaxed, setting the rifle aside as he recognized little Paco. He looked worried, but Paco usually carried such an expression. He faced Banner now, hat in hand.

'There is a man at the cantina, *señor,* He looks for you. Says there is trouble at the Pine Tree rancho. He says Tina sends him.'

'What does this man look like, Paco?'

'Not like the others, *señor.* This man is young. A boy only. He is someone that I like.'

'I trust your judgement, Paco. He have a name?'

'*Si,* but he says that it will mean nothing to you. He works for a man called Cody. I think that is a name I have heard before.'

'You have, Paco. He was in the cantina with another two men the last time I was in there. Did the boy say what kind of trouble they had at Pine Tree?'

'Something about a missing boy, *señor*. I think this is not a good thing.'

'You are right,' Banner said flatly. 'It is not a good thing. I will meet up with this boy, find out what he knows.'

'I will wait for you, *señor*,' Paco said proudly. 'We will ride back to my cantina together.'

Banner splashed water from the little stream into his face to wash away the grime of working in the mine. 'That may not be a good idea, Paco. Someone may have followed you here and be waiting for us along the way. You'll be safer travelling on your own.'

'You think I have been used to lead someone to you, *señor?* The boy has an honest face. It is hard to believe.'

'It's just a feeling I have, Paco, but my hunches have kept me alive so far so I'll keep going along with them. They may be using the boy, too, without him being aware of it.'

Paco shook his head sadly. 'This is

not a good thing, *señor*. To think that I should lead them to you. Paco must make penance.'

'No harm done, Paco. You will ride back alone to the cantina, keep the boy there if you can. If there is someone following you he won't risk me hearing a shot, so you'll be safe to go back home. I won't be far behind.'

Satisfied, Paco mounted his little burro. The *señor* was not angry with him, although he had every right to be.

'One other thing, Paco,' Banner said softly. 'You have been a friend, a good friend. I will be leaving here soon, and the mine will be yours. It will not make you rich but perhaps it will help you improve your business.' Paco nodded. The *señor* was too generous, but it would be an insult to say no, would it not?

Quickly Banner saddled the black. Somewhere in those rocks below, a killer would be waiting for him. He was sure of it. And he had a pretty good idea who it would be. He had walked away from Buckman with $10,000 for doing a job that Jack Stagg couldn't handle. And he had braced the half-breed in front of Buckman and Cody. Neither fact would sit well with the Yaqui half-breed. Well, it had to come to this sooner or later. There was no dodging that fact. He moved the black out of sight before changing into moccasins.

Banner jacked a shell into the chamber of his Winchester before selecting a place in the rocks above the mine entrance. If his guess was right and Stagg was down there, he would watch Paco until the little Mexican was out of sight and wait for Banner. Well, he would have a long wait. Banner settled himself comfortably among the rocks. Sometime, Stagg would have to come looking for him. With a little luck it wouldn't take too long. Within an hour or so Stagg would realize that there was the possibility of another trail leading away from the mine.

An hour passed slowly but Banner wasn't aware of it. He had been playing this game for too long. A sudden movement caught his eye, and he allowed himself a half-grin as he spotted Stagg creeping between the rocks. Was he alone? He thought so, but wanted to be certain. There weren't many men who liked working with Stagg. He liked more than his share of the money. Stagg was at the mine entrance now, looking inside, listening for the sounds of Banner working. Nothing. There was no sign of Banner's horse, either. That could only mean one thing: there was another trail out of this place and Banner had taken it.

He smiled. It meant Banner had a few more hours left to live, that was all. He would reach the border before him and be waiting at the crossing. His first shot would put Banner out of action and he would finish the job slowly with his knife, he promised himself.

'You'd never make a living fighting

Comanches, Stagg.'

The suddenness of the words startled Stagg. He leapt into the mine entrance, his heart pounding. How had Banner known he was waiting down there for him? A hunch? Instinct? It didn't matter. Banner knew, and he had fooled him. Yet the question bugged him. 'How did you know, Banner?'

'It was just a matter of time, Stagg. I made you back down, and everyone talked about it. You had to settle the score. Only Paco knows about this place. He's the only one who could lead you here. That boy back at the cantina, was he part of your plan?'

'He came in handy. When I heard he was being sent to Mexico to look for you I decided to trail along behind. Cody told him where to come, but he wasn't about to give me that information.'

'What about the boy, Stagg? Has something happened to him?'

Stagg laughed. 'There's nothing you can

do about it, Banner. It's too late for him and it's too late for you. I'm going to bury you, Banner.' It was Banner's turn to laugh as he moved swiftly and silently from his hiding place, using all available cover until he was facing the mine entrance.

'No, Stagg. I'm going to bury you unless you want to throw your guns out now. It's your choice. First you tell me about the boy.'

'The Comanches've got him again, Banner. Feel like going back to the stronghold after him? Maybe you'll get lucky again, but I doubt it. There is nothing you or anyone else can do about him, Banner. Hell, he was just another half-breed. Who cares about him?'

Banner's shot flicked rock splinters at his face and he stepped back quickly. He had Banner located now, behind that big rock facing the mine entrance. To get a good clear shot at Stagg, he would have to step out a little, enough for Stagg to take him out. The half-breed grinned. Banner wasn't as clever as he thought he was. Stagg could have taken him a long time ago if Buckman hadn't kept him on a tight rein.

'Last chance, Stagg. Are you coming out or do you want to die right there?'

'There's no way you can kill me, Banner, without stepping out from behind that rock. I can wait that long to kill you.'

'You made the decision, Stagg. Remember that.'

Banner's shot splintered the post near Stagg's left side. He grinned again. The wrong angle. The best Banner could hope for was a wayward slug bouncing off the mine shaft. It wasn't much of a hope. Another slug slammed into the mine support. The slugs were coming thick and fast now, but nowhere near him. The grin froze on his face. What the hell was Banner up to? Did he think to frighten him out with all that lead? For a moment the thought of rushing out while Banner was reloading the rifle crossed his mind, but he quashed it quickly. Banner still had a pistol, and a big reputation with it.

He could wait. Banner wasn't hurting him with all that lead he was throwing about, and sooner or later it had to run out. Then ... the lead was coming in his direction again, and he heard a sudden rumble, as if the mountain above him was making some kind of protest. Well, let it protest to Banner; he was the one doing all the shooting. He wasn't about to do harm to anyone until Banner ran out of lead or stepped into sight.

'Last chance, Stagg,' Banner shouted.

'Come and get me, Banner. If you've got the nerve.'

'Goodbye, Stagg,' Banner said quietly, pumping two more shots into the mine support.

'You are going to have to shoot a lot better than that to get me, Banner.'

'My shots went just where I wanted them to go, Stagg,' Banner said softly, moving slowly into view, the rifle hanging loose at his side. For a second, Stagg hesitated. Another of Banner's tricks. It was either a ruse or Banner was a fool. A fool. That had to be it. It was just him and Banner now, just as he had always known it would be. Banner was about to die and it was a good feeling.

The sudden splintering of the timbers unnerved him as he started to lift his rifle. Damn Banner. He had fooled him again. He intended this mine to be his grave. None of his shots had been meant for him. All of Banner's shots had been aimed at the mine supports. This was Banner's mine. He knew its strengths and its weaknesses. Maybe he had already weakened some of those timbers while Jack Stagg had been waiting down the trail for him.

He forced his suddenly weak legs to move towards the entrance, but he could already feel the mountain starting to close in on him. His screams were lost in the rumble of falling rocks as the mountain came down.

Banner stood impassive as the mountain settled back to its natural state. He had felt that it had never liked his intrusion anyway. Little Paco wouldn't have his silver mine after all, but some extra pesos would ease some of the pain for him. Only after the mountain was quiet did he go after the black and step into the saddle. Something had happened to Bobby and he didn't like the sound of it. Stagg had hinted that the boy was dead or heading back for the stronghold. Would Two Ponies break his word to Banner? He doubted it. But if he had the Comanche would find themselves facing a foe more terrible than even they could imagine.

Banner entered the back door of Paco's cantina quietly, his mind and body alert for trouble. The boy, just as Paco had described him, stood talking to Paco. The boy had been right—his name wouldn't have meant anything to Banner, but he had seen him at Pine Tree on his brief visits there. He let the door close noisily behind him, catching the boy's attention.

He looked relieved. 'The name is Billy Todd, Mr Banner. Cody sent me to find you. They need help back at Pine Tree. Bobby's missing. No sign of him anyplace. We think maybe the Comanche got him. What would the Comanche want with a five-year-old kid, Mr Banner?'

Banner knew the answer to that one, but didn't even want to think about it. Two Ponies wouldn't go back on his word. He was sure of it. 'What makes anyone think it was Comanche took the boy?' he asked quietly.

'Someone found a feather near the stables. Seemed to think it was Comanche, I wouldn't know, Mr Banner. I've never been that close to a Comanche. Wouldn't want to.'

'Ride back to Pine Tree. Tell Cody I'll be along. Maybe I'll catch up with you along the way.'

'I'm in no hurry to face Cody again,

Mr Banner. He's in a bad mood. Can't blame him, I guess. But things would go a lot easier for me if I was to ride in with you.'

Banner shook his head. 'I had a bit of trouble back there. There may be more ahead. It's best if I travel alone.' He turned his attention to Paco. 'Sorry, amigo. You lost your mine. The mountain came down on it.'

Paco nodded sagely. 'Mountains do that sometimes, *señor*. I trust the mountain will not be lonely without you.'

'It's got company,' Banner said, moving towards the door.

17

Banner rode slowly, his face thoughtful. Bobby missing! A little five-year-old boy out there alone in a big hostile land. Lost or dead? Stagg had implied that, too. The thought sickened him. He had fought against it but the kid had got to him. Bobby had touched him in a way that no one had for a long time; but his sister was dead. Was history about to repeat itself? It had a habit of doing that.

The girl had been right all along but he hadn't listened. They should never have left the cabin. They had all been safe up there. No threat from the Comanche or anyone else. It was a good place for a kid to grow up. The books in the cabin would have provided all the education the boy would need. Outside the cabin, Banner could have taught him everything he would need to know about the country. Banner would have learned a lot, too ... he already had.

The sound of a galloping horse disturbed his thoughts. Without even thinking about it, as if it had a life of its own, the big black Colt had slipped into his hand as he reined his horse.

The man galloping towards him was an elderly Mexican, his seat unsteady on the galloping horse. A burro was far more suitable for him. Horses frightened him. They were temperamental creatures, not reliable like a burro. The horse passed Banner before he finally managed to bring it to a stop. He waited for Banner to catch up, afraid to risk turning the animal in case it ran off with him again.

'I am not a good rider, *señor*,' he confessed quickly. 'But Paco said it was urgent that I should catch up with you. This I could not do on a burro.'

He stopped talking and looked frightened as his horse moved restlessly.

'Paco said I should speak with you, *señor*. He said that you are looking for a missing boy. Perhaps I can help.'

The breath caught in Banner's throat. Bad news? He felt a sudden tension in his stomach. Had the little Mexican seen something that he didn't really want to disclose? It looked that way. The little Mexican was hesitant, too hesitant. He looked guilty.

'I am not proud of myself, *señor*,' Manuel said slowly. 'When the man came to us with the little boy, I was afraid. Paco is a hero, but I am a coward,' he admitted sadly.

Banner felt the anger boil up in him, but it was no use in pushing the little Mexican. He would only frighten him. He was hanging his head in shame now.

'I should not have taken the money, *señor*, but I was afraid, and I wanted to come back to Mexico with my family.

Two hundred dollars is a lot of money for one such as me. When the tall man suggested that I come back to Mexico I listened to his words. Now I am ashamed. It is not right that a child should be apart from his family, but the man said that the boy would be killed if I did not take him with me back to Mexico.

'I did not wish any harm to come to the boy, *señor*, so I did as the man said I should. I thought I should speak with Paco, seek his advice. He told me I should ride after you, and tell you what I have done. I am sorry, *señor*. But I did not know what else to do.'

'This man who gave the boy to you, what did he look like?'

'Tall, *señor*, with a scar on his cheek. His left cheek, I think.'

'Where is the boy now?'

'He is safe back at Paco's cantina. I would like you to take the money back for me, *señor*. I should not have accepted it, but I was afraid.'

Banner smiled one of his rare smiles. Bobby was safe.

'Tell me about the boy. What does he look like?'

'Like one of my own children, *señor*, but he does not speak my language, only American and a language I do not understand.'

Banner's grin broadened. Comanche. That was the language that the little Mexican could not understand. It was Bobby. 'Keep the money, amigo. I think you have earned it. There will be a little something extra for you when you get back to Paco's.'

Wheeling the black, he set off in a full gallop back towards the cantina, as happy to see the boy again as Bobby would be to see him. The smile was on his face as he dismounted at a run outside Paco's cantina. Bobby was there, sad-faced and confused among a bunch of fussing women. He hadn't even noticed Banner's arrival until the tall man spoke.

'Looks like I can't leave you alone for a minute without you getting into some kind of trouble.'

Bobby spun around, his face wreathed in smiles. He was no longer alone and afraid among strangers. Banner had found him, just as he had always known he would. He rushed into his arms, happy as Banner lifted him high before hugging him close. Paco was astonished to see something akin to tears in Banner's eyes. It was good to see the *señor* so happy, but someone had stolen the boy from his mother and there would be a price to pay. The *señor* would make sure of that. Paco shivered. It would be a terrible price that Señor Banner would demand.

'Let's go home, Bobby,' Banner said gently. 'There's someone waiting to see you.'

'Back to the cabin, Matt?' the boy asked, a plea in his voice.

'Not yet, but soon,' Banner promised. Bobby had made the decisions that he and

Tina had been afraid to make. He smiled wryly. Perhaps they should let Bobby make all their decisions for them. He wondered if Ghost Warrior was smiling, too, wherever he was. It looked as if he was going to get his wish, after all.

He lifted the boy into the black's saddle before mounting himself. It was a long ride back to Pine Tree and there wouldn't be many stops along the way. Tina would be frantic with worry. The best medicine for that would be to reunite her with her son as soon as possible.

Grim-faced, he listened to the story of how two men had come to Pine Tree and stolen the boy. The tall man with the cruel face had threatened the boy with a knife, should he cry out. This was the man who had frightened him most.

Banner touched the boy's cheek with a soothing, gentle hand. 'He won't frighten you any more, Bobby. He can't hurt anyone ever again.'

'I'm not afraid any more, Matt. You

won't let anyone hurt me again.'

Banner smiled, before letting his face settle back into his usual grim expression. Jack Stagg hadn't been acting alone. He had been following orders, and Banner knew just who had given those orders. Bobby fell asleep before they reached the Rio, worn out by relief at seeing Banner, and his own constant chatter. For a moment, Banner had considered stopping to let the boy get some proper sleep but decided against it. At the moment he felt more secure in Banner's arms. Nothing could hurt him there, no nightmares or the face of Jack Stagg to haunt him. Banner had watched the mountain come down on Jack Stagg and had felt guilty, but no longer.

It was early morning when they arrived at Pine Tree. The place was almost deserted, but he was greeted by Billy Todd. The youth had been keeping an eye open for him. He gave a wild rebel yell as he spotted Bobby sitting on the saddle before Banner.

'How did you find him? We've had forty men scouring the country for him.'

'It's a long story,' Banner told him. 'I'll tell you another time. Where's Tina and Cody?'

'Over at the major's place. Some kind of powwow. Seems the major is in a hurry to set up a wedding date.' He spat into the dust. 'You gonna do something about that, Banner?'

'Been thinking along those lines,' Banner admitted dryly. 'Take care of the boy for me, Billy, until I get back.'

'Be careful, Banner. I haven't seen Jack Stagg around and that's when he's most dangerous.'

'I left him buried under a mountain in Mexico. He trailed you to Paco's cantina before tagging along behind Paco until he found me.'

Billy grinned. 'Hope you let him live long enough to regret it? Sorry, Banner, I never figured on anyone following me.'

'Had to happen sooner or later,' Banner

said, handing the boy down.

'He'll be here when you get back,' Todd promised. 'I'm not going to take my eyes off him.'

Banner dismounted outside the ranch-house. As usual, the major had the floor. 'We have to face the facts, Tina. The boy is either dead or a prisoner of the Comanche. I'm sorry to be so blunt but we have scoured the country and there isn't a sign of him. I think it's best that we get on with our lives. I can arrange for us to be married next week, whichever day you choose.'

Tina faced him, proud and defiant. 'I don't believe my son is dead, Major. He is out there somewhere, and Banner will find him, no matter how long it takes.'

'I haven't got the kind of money it would take to hire Banner, Tina. And neither do you. The bank won't extend you any more credit. You already owe too much. When we are married, I'll pay off your bank loan and all your problems will be solved.'

'And just forget I had a son, is that it, Major? No matter where my son is Banner will go after him, and it won't cost me a cent. Banner paid off my bank debt with the money you gave him. He told me once that he thought you and he were a lot alike. He was wrong: you are not fit to clean his boots.

'It has taken a long time but I've finally come to my senses. If I had kept hold of Banner the way I should, Bobby wouldn't be missing now. I'm not going to marry you, Major, next week or ever. Perhaps you think you can hold me to my grandmother's promise, but you can't. I may feel guilty for a long time but I'll learn to live with it. I owe that to my son and Banner. I owe it to the boy's father, too. It was his wish that Banner care for his son, knowing that Banner wouldn't deny the boy his heritage.'

Her eyes swept over the men assembled in the major's house, knowing the impact her next words would cause. 'I haven't been in Mexico for the past nine years as the major would have you believe. I was a prisoner of the Comanche in the Lost River country until Banner came and rescued me. I was Ghost Warrior's woman. Bobby is his son.'

She felt a certain satisfaction as the sudden silence filled the room.

There it was out in the open and it was a good feeling. She watched the anger bloom on Buckman's face. Her announcement had blown away all his plans. Banner was right. No one could live a lie forever. It was like trying to hold a snake by its tail. Sooner or later the head would have to come around and bite you. She couldn't, didn't, want to live with that kind of tension. It wasn't fair to Bobby or her.

Tina felt Cody move forward to give her support with a hand on her shoulder. He would stand by her as she had always known he would, but he could never offer the kind of strength that Banner had. Buckman would have to think twice before threatening her if Matt were here. But he wasn't. Where was he? Billy Todd should have found him by now, and aboard that big black of his should have been back here. Where was he? Didn't he know how much she needed him?

Buckman's face, bloated with anger, hovered over her. Tina's confession about being the wife of Ghost Warrior had upset all his plans. No one would ever take a squawman seriously. 'You've lost the boy, Tina, and you are going to lose Pine Tree. All the land around here will belong to me. You'll have nothing.'

'I have already lived with nothing, Buckman. As far as I am concerned you can own the whole of Texas. All I care about is a cabin in the mountains. When Banner finds Bobby, I intend going back to that cabin. I want to hear the song of the first bird in spring, and watch the leaves turn to gold in the Fall. Those are the kind of things that money can't buy, Major, so you wouldn't be interested.'

He smiled. 'You think Banner and your half-breed son will be with you, Tina? You're wrong. You'll be alone. All alone. Jack Stagg had some personal business in Mexico. Billy Todd will have helped him find the man he was looking for by now.'

His smile broadened at the fearful look on Tina's face. Banner wouldn't be expecting Stagg or anyone else waiting in ambush for him. He would be killed. She felt Cody's reassuring hand on her shoulder again.

'Don't worry about Banner, Tina. He can smell a skunk like Stagg a mile off. I'll make you a bet, Buckman; I'll bet two months' wages that Banner will walk through that door behind me before Stagg does.'

'You have a bet, Cody,' Buckman said. 'By now Banner is dead.'

'Banner isn't an easy man to kill.

Major. Ghost Warrior and his Comanches found that out the hard way,' Tina said, advancing on him, facing him unafraid. 'Banner is coming, Buckman. There is no man on this earth can stop him. He's close by. I always know when he's near. I can sense his presence. To the Comanche he is the most terrifying man that ever lived, and you are going to find out why they think of him that way.'

Buckman's hand lashed out, leaving a vivid mark on her face. Cody moved forward, his face tight with anger, but she stopped him with a smile.

'You ever wonder how a condemned man feels, Cody? First they start counting the days, then the hours, the minutes, and finally the seconds. Buckman is going to feel that way. In one way I suppose it's worse than the actual execution. I think you had better start counting, Major.'

Was there any truth in what she said, he wondered? Could Banner escape Jack Stagg? Stagg was a half-breed Yaqui but Banner had been fighting full-blood Comanches for more years than he cared to remember. He had killed Ghost Warrior in hand-to-hand combat. But what the hell. Even if Banner got by Jack Stagg, he would still be living on borrowed time. He would find himself with a bounty on his head. And that would be the end of Banner. He had enough men working for him to take care of Banner. But how many of his men would be willing to go up against him?

For the first time he was beginning to experience doubts and didn't like it. Big, powerful men should never feel threatened. He could buy and sell men as he chose. Banner was the only man he had ever known who didn't have a price.

He looked around at the other men in the room. Four of his men, but no one he could trust, apart from Brody. Brody had helped Stagg kidnap and murder the boy. That gave him a hold over the man. Brody would have to do as he was told. Still he wished Stagg was with him. Even the half-breed's presence intimidated people. They all knew what he was capable of.

There was a half-amused glint in Tina's eyes as she watched the doubt spread over his face. Damn her! She would come begging to him before this was all over. She would have nothing. He would destroy her and enjoy doing it. Stagg would be turned loose on anyone who dared stand in his way.

He forced a smile on to his dry lips again. 'Stagg will be back soon. I'll have him tell you how Banner died, screaming for mercy.'

She stepped forward, laughing in his face. 'You won't be seeing Jack Stagg again, except in Hell.'

'And that may be sooner than you think,' Banner said coldly, stepping into the room. His bleak eyes swept over Buckman's men before settling on Tina. The briefest of smiles touched his lips. 'Bobby's safe back at Pine Tree.'

One of Buckman's men moved uncomfortably and Banner turned his attention to him, his hand resting on his gunbutt. Brody lifted his hands high. 'You got no quarrel with me, Banner. You owe me. I'm the reason the kid is still alive, the only reason. Stagg was all set to kill him, but I talked him out of it. I told him I knew of a good place to get rid of him, a place where he would never be found. Said it was best that I do the job alone for an extra fifty bucks. Stagg looked forward to killing him, until I pointed out that if anyone suspected any foul play he would be the first one they looked at. That made sense to him. It would be best if he were at the dance in plain sight. His reputation wouldn't be much use to him if anyone thought he had murdered a kid. There wouldn't be enough bullets in his gun to stop a lynch mob and no place to hide from something like that. Every man and woman in the country would be looking for him.'

He stopped talking, his throat suddenly dry. Banner's expression hadn't changed. He swallowed hard. Somehow he had to convince Banner. 'I knew of a Mexican family, heard him talking of returning to Mexico as soon as he got enough pesos together. They already had half-a-dozen kids so I figured another one wouldn't make much difference. The kid looked Mexican. We didn't know about the boy being Ghost Warrior's son until a few minutes ago. That was Buckman's big secret. I gave the Mex two hundred dollars to take the boy with him, provided they left that night. It was all I could think of. It wasn't safe around here for the kid, and I didn't want him killed. It was the best I could do. If you want to blow my head off for that, then go ahead.'

Still nothing had changed in Banner's face. 'Just one thing before you leave, mister. Who gave the orders for killing Bobby?'

Brody started breathing deeply again.

Banner had said he could leave. That was good enough for him. There was no future around here for him, anyway. 'Buckman, I guess. Stagg never did anything without orders from the major. Buckman didn't like the idea of having the kid around. I didn't know why until the girl told us about being the wife of Ghost Warrior and blew his secret. It made sense then, a lot of sense. No one was going to vote for a squawman. The major wanted public office. Having a half-breed for a son would put a crimp in his ambitions.' He hesitated. 'I figure you owe me something, Banner. Just a small favour; I'd like to see you kill Buckman before I leave. If you were around I'd have brought the kid right to you. I want you to believe that.'

'I believe it. But I don't know about the other thing. Buckman hasn't got the guts to face a man with a gun. He buys his killings. It doesn't matter much to him. He isn't pulling a trigger. Tell me, Brody, how much do you reckon the major's life is worth?'

'Once this story gets out, I'd say about one cent.'

Banner advanced on Buckman slowly, sending a chill through the big man. He could never hope to match Banner with a gun. 'Hear that, Major? Your man there thinks your life is worth one cent. I think you are over-priced. You won't have much more than that when you ride away from here, if I let you ride away.'

Buckman made a last attempt at defiance. Banner was here and that could mean only one thing: Stagg was dead. He was alone, but only for a moment. The money he had in the safe would hire more guns. Banner had managed to escape Stagg, and maybe he could run Buckman out, but he would be back with enough guns to rule this whole place again. Every man around here would be on his payroll. His mouth twisted. 'I'll be back, Banner. You can bet on that.'

He moved towards the safe but Banner was standing before him. 'You don't listen very good, do you, Buckman? Your stableman has a horse already saddled. He's all you've got, that and what you have in your pocket. The money in the safe belongs to the people you robbed when you stole their land. If I ever see you again, I'll kill you. I made the same promise to Jack Stagg, remember? I'm here. He's not.'

His fist lashed out suddenly, slamming into Buckman's face, driving him backwards. 'I think you should have something to remember me by, Major. I want other people to be able to recognize you and remember the story of a man who tried to have a five-year-old boy murdered.'

His left fist smashed into Buckman's gut, driving the wind from his body. Soft. Buckman had spent too much time sitting and drinking brandy.

His right ripped the major's brow wide open. Good. That would leave a scar, something for people to remember and recall the story of the man who had hired a half-breed Yaqui to kill a boy. Coldly, he destroyed Buckman, every punch ripping into the big man's face. There would be a lot of scars. One of the few punches Buckman had caught him with had ripped his eyebrow, but it was nothing a few stitches wouldn't cure. Finally satisfied, he stepped back, letting Buckman sag to the floor. He nodded to Brody. 'I think the major will need a little help getting on his horse.'

Brody grinned as he moved forward. Banner hadn't just beaten Buckman, he had destroyed him. All Buckman's confidence, pride and arrogance had disappeared. He would never be the same again. He would never again give an order, never look another man in the face. For the rest of his life he would wonder if there was another Banner waiting around the next corner for him, or even the real one.

Banner watched Buckman's men take him from the ranch-house. It was over, or was it just a beginning for him? Hell, it wasn't going to be easy, but he would handle it. Was she ready to take a chance on someone like him? It would be a big gamble for her. Half of his life had been spent on his own. No one to care for or care about, but maybe it was time for a change. His eyes found hers.

'I'm sorry you had to see that,' he said quietly.

'I'm not. It was something you had to do, Matt. I understand that.'

She took his hand gently. It felt good. It was even better when she stretched up to kiss him. 'I want to see spring in our valley, Matt. Just you, Bobby and me. We are all we will ever need.'

This Large Print Book for the Partially sighted, who cannot read normal print, is published under the auspices of

THE ULVERSCROFT FOUNDATION